Sam pulled Serena closer to his lean, hard body....

She didn't respond this way to other men.

"There's something about you," he said after a long moment, "that makes me forget every promise I made to myself. Something that completely destroys my willpower."

"Trust me," she said after moistening her tender lips. "I know the feeling."

"There's something I need to talk to you about," he said, lifting his head.

This was definitely not the time to talk about anything important. She could barely speak, much less think clearly. Still, she was curious. She studied his face. That lost look was in his eyes again—the one that sneaked behind the few defenses she had left against him. There was a sadness in Sam she didn't understand and didn't know how to alleviate.

Realizing she was still standing in his arms, their bodies still intimately pressed together, she eased away from him. "We'll talk tomorrow...."

Dear Reader,

Many people read romance novels for the unforgettable heroes that capture our hearts and stay with us long after the last page is read. But to give all the credit for the success of this genre to these handsome hunks is to underestimate the value of the heart of a romance: the heroine.

"Heroes are fantasy material, but for me, the heroines are much more grounded in real life," says Susan Mallery, bestselling author of this month's *Shelter in a Soldier's Arms*. "For me, the heroine is at the center of the story. I want to write and read about women who are intelligent, funny and determined."

Gina Wilkins's *The Stranger in Room 205* features a beautiful newspaper proprietor who discovers an amnesiac in her backyard and finds herself in an adventure of a lifetime! And don't miss *The M.D. Meets His Match* in Hades, Alaska, where Marie Ferrarella's snowbound heroine unexpectedly finds romance that is sure to heat up the bitter cold....

Peggy Webb delivers an *Invitation to a Wedding;* when the heroine is rescued from marrying the wrong man, could a long-lost friend end up being Mr. Right? Sparks fly in Lisette Belisle's novel when the heroine, raising *Her Sister's Secret Son,* meets a mysterious man who claims to be the boy's father! And in Patricia McLinn's *Almost a Bride,* a rancher desperate to save her ranch enters into a marriage of convenience, but with temptation as her bed partner, life becomes a minefield of desire.

Special Edition is proud to publish novels featuring strong, admirable heroines struggling to balance life, love and family and making dreams come true. Enjoy! And look inside for details about our Silhouette Makes You a Star contest.

Best,

Karen Taylor Richman, Senior Editor

Please address questions and book requests to:
Silhouette Reader Service
U.S.: 3010 Walden Ave., P.O. Box 1325, Buffalo, NY 14269
Canadian: P.O. Box 609, Fort Erie, Ont. L2A 5X3

The Stranger in Room 205

GINA WILKINS

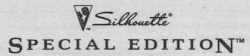

Silhouette®

SPECIAL EDITION™

Published by Silhouette Books

America's Publisher of Contemporary Romance

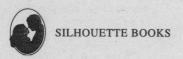 SILHOUETTE BOOKS

ISBN 0-373-24399-5

THE STRANGER IN ROOM 205

Visit Silhouette at www.eHarlequin.com

Printed in U.S.A.

GINA WILKINS

is a bestselling and award-winning author who has written more than fifty books for Harlequin and Silhouette Books. She credits her successful career in romance to her long, happy marriage and her three "extraordinary" children.

A lifelong resident of central Arkansas, Ms. Wilkins sold her first book to Harlequin in 1987 and has been writing full-time since. She has appeared on the Waldenbooks, B. Dalton and *USA Today* bestseller lists. She is a three-time recipient of the Maggie Award for Excellence, sponsored by Georgia Romance Writers, and has won several awards from the reviewers of *Romantic Times Magazine*.

Chapter One

"Sir? Are you awake? Can you hear me?"

The woman's voice was nice, but muffled, and there was a funny buzzing noise underlying it. Like static, he thought without opening his eyes. The darkness was intense, cocooning him like a warm, heavy comforter. He wanted to wrap it more tightly around himself and drift back into oblivion, but the voice intruded again.

"I know you're in pain, but you really should try to open your eyes," the woman advised him. "You need to let us know you're awake."

He wanted to tell her to leave him alone. He was tired. He would appreciate it if she went away and let him rest. He opened his mouth to tell her so, but only a hoarse croak emerged from his dry throat.

"Oh, good, you *are* waking up. Can you tell me your name?"

It seemed there would be no rest for him until he acknowledged her. Maybe if he opened his eyes—just for a moment—she'd go away. He forced his lids apart, then groaned when light assaulted his pupils, causing an eruption of pain inside his head.

He glared at the woman leaning into his face. This was her fault. She'd nagged him out of the tranquil darkness and brought this pounding to his temples. All in all, he thought it would be better if he went back to sleep.

"Oh, no, you don't," she said. "Wake up and tell me your name. I want to know you're all right before I leave you here."

Leave him *where?* Suddenly he realized that he hadn't the faintest idea where he was. He opened his eyes again and tried to ask, but the results of his attempt at speech were pathetic. Sounded like a bullfrog had mistaken his tongue for a lily pad. The woman touched his face. Her hand was cool. Soft. Felt good. Too bad about her face, though. It kept …changing. Four eyes, then three, then four again. They were rather pretty eyes. Blue. Or maybe green. However many of them she had.

He allowed his own to close again, welcoming the relief of the darkness. The light was too painful to deal with for now.

"Sir? Before you go to sleep again, isn't there someone you'd like me to call? Your family, perhaps?"

His family? Did he *have* a family? Funny—at the moment, he couldn't remember. Probably because the pain drowned out everything else. It seemed so much easier to slip away from it. He allowed himself to do just that.

* * *

"He's out again." Serena sighed and sat back in the straight chair beside the wounded man's bed. She was alone in the small hospital room with him, and she glanced at her watch, thinking of the hour that had passed since he'd been brought to the hospital by ambulance, with her following in her own car. The stranger had drifted in and out of consciousness several times, but never fully enough to really consider him awake.

She'd missed her morning meeting, of course. She simply hadn't been able to abandon this poor guy until she was reassured that there was someone who knew or cared where and how he was. He'd had the misfortune to be brought in at almost the same time a bus full of teenagers returning from a church-sponsored field trip had run off the road and into a ditch on the way home. None of the passengers was critically injured—broken bones and abrasions the most severe consequences of the accident—but the little hospital was in chaos with hysterical adolescents and parents crowding the hallways. Her stranger, as she'd taken to calling him until she had a better name for him, had been examined, pronounced in fair condition except for a concussion and left in this room until one of the overwhelmed small staff had time to deal with him more fully.

Serena knew she had no obligation to sit by his side, since she had done no more than find him in a ditch and summon help for him, but something kept her there. That overdeveloped sense of responsibility of hers, most likely. It seemed like most of her life was spent doing things she felt obligated to do, rather than things she truly wanted to do.

She was becoming concerned about his continued unconsciousness. Sure, he was wired to all sorts of monitors and such, but was anyone really keeping a close eye on him with everything going on outside this room? She could hear an overwrought parent shouting down the hall, demanding attention for his daughter even as an exasperated nurse tried to assure him that someone would be with him as soon as possible. The guy sounded like Red Tucker, Serena thought with a wince, pitying the poor nurse. Everyone knew Red had a temper that matched his nickname, and a severe patience deficiency to boot.

As if the noise outside had disturbed his fitful sleep, her stranger muttered something, bringing Serena's attention back to him. She studied his face curiously. Though presently disfigured with swelling and bruises, she would bet his features were usually quite handsome. His hair, when clean and styled, was probably a rich gold, and the eyes she had seen so briefly were a bright blue. He was slim and fit, probably in his early thirties—only a year or two older than herself, she would guess. His hands were well-tended, except for the abraded knuckles that indicated he'd fought back when he'd suffered the vicious beating that had landed him here. His nails were clean and neatly trimmed. She doubted that he'd ever done much manual labor.

He wore no watch or other jewelry, had been dressed only in a ripped pullover and a pair of jeans, had carried nothing in his pockets and had worn no shoes or socks. If robbery had been the motive for the vicious beating, his attacker had taken nearly everything. She didn't recognize this man and neither had anyone else who'd seen him so far, which was unusual for such a small community. So where had he come from? What had he been doing on the side of a gravel road that led nowhere outside of this off-the-beaten-path little Arkansas town?

Someone opened the door behind her. She expected to see a doctor or a nurse when she looked around, but discovered Dan Meadows walking in, instead. "I wondered when someone would get around to calling the police," she murmured.

"'Evening, Serena," the chief of police said. He showed no surprise at seeing her there, which meant he'd already talked to someone outside. "Heard you found a wounded stray behind your house."

She tucked a strand of her chin-length brown hair behind her ear and nodded. "He was in the ditch beside Bullock Lake Road. My sister's dog got out of my yard and I was chasing him when I found this man lying facedown in the grass."

A tough-looking, slow-talking man in his mid-thirties, Dan crossed the room with his trademark rolling amble and studied the man in the bed. "I've never seen him before."

"Neither have I. I have a feeling he's not from around here."

"Got any other hunches you'd like to share with me?"

She shook her head. "I'm afraid not. I can't imagine what he was doing there. There was no ID on him—or anywhere around him in the ditch. I looked."

"Looks like someone beat the hell out of him."

"Apparently. Dr. Frank said he has a concussion, a few broken ribs, a badly sprained wrist and several painful cuts and bruises."

"Stitched up his head, did they?"

"He had a deep cut to the scalp at his right temple. It took six stitches to close it."

Dan nodded, still looking at the man on the bed. "Has he been awake?"

"Not for more than seconds at a time. I thought he was waking up a few minutes ago, but he drifted off again. They've pumped him full of antibiotics and who knows what else. I suppose the drugs could be affecting him."

"More likely the concussion. LuWanda said she'd be in to check on him as soon as she gets Red Tucker calmed down. I'd better get out there and help her. Nothing like a hospital full of panicky parents to keep everyone hopping."

"Thank God none of the students was seriously injured."

"Yeah. My niece was on that bus," Dan admitted with a grimace. "Scared the stuffing out of me when I heard about it."

"Polly's okay?"

"She's fine. Got herself a bloody nose and a black eye, but she'll be okay once she gets over the scare."

"I'm glad to hear it."

"Yeah. By the way, your scoop girl's out there making a nuisance of herself. Want me to send her in to keep you company?"

She smiled and shook her head. "Let Lindsey do her job."

"Asking all the parents how it feels to almost lose a child in a bus accident? Hell of a job, if you ask me."

Dan had never made any secret of his opinion of the reporters who worked for the *Evening Star,* the newspaper Serena's great-grandfather had started, and which she now owned through a set of circumstances that still bewildered her. Before she could defend the importance of the press to him—for perhaps the thousandth time—an outburst in the hallway caught their attention.

Dan sighed. "Sounds like Red's getting wound up again. I'd better go give LuWanda a hand with him. You going to stay around awhile?"

She nodded. "I feel as though I should stay until things calm down a bit and someone has time to spend with this poor man."

"'This poor man?'" Dan's expression was quizzical. "You know something about him that I don't?"

"No, of course not. I just—well, you know. I found him and now I feel sort of responsible for him."

"Mmm. That's the kind of thinking that gets well-intentioned folks in trouble. Better find out who he is before you adopt him."

Fully aware that Dan was always suspicious of outsiders in his town and would be particularly wary of anyone who showed up under these circumstances, Serena nodded. She was as vigilant as Dan about keeping their hometown free from the crimes that had taken hold in so many places even as small and unremarkable as this.

Dan glanced again at the man in the bed on his way out of the room. "Have someone call me when he wakes up, will you? I have a few questions for him."

Serena watched him leave. He left the door open a couple of inches, so she could hear him speaking in his measured, authoritative manner, his voice fading as he moved away with Red Tucker and whoever else had been in the hallway outside the room. And then she ran a hand through her hair again and turned to keep watch over the man in the bed—only to find that his eyes were open and focused intently on her face.

"Oh. So you're awake again. Are you able yet to talk to the chief of police, or would you like me to give you a few minutes before I call him back in?"

The woman was sitting in a chair very close to the narrow bed on which he found himself. She leaned slightly toward him as she spoke, and there appeared to be concern in her eyes. He knew those eyes. Blue. Or maybe green. Pretty. There were only two of them this time. One nose. One mouth. All very nicely arranged in an oval face framed in a soft brown bob. Whatever had happened to him—and he was awake enough to realize that he was lying in a hospital room—he was still able to recognize that this was a very attractive woman. He found that observation reassuring. He couldn't be damaged too badly if he was still interested in the opposite sex.

"Sir?" she repeated when he continued to stare at her rather than answering. "Did you hear me? Can you speak to me?"

He blinked, trying to recall what she'd said. Something about…police? He frowned, then winced when his swollen, sore face rebelled against the expression. "Uh—yeah, I can hear you," he managed to say, his voice gruff, as if it hadn't been used in a long time.

The sound of it seemed to encourage her. "How do you feel?"

The only appropriate phrase he could come up with in answer seemed inappropriate for mixed company. He settled for, "Not great."

"I don't doubt it. You have several very painful injuries, but the doctor said you'll be fine. Things are rather hectic here tonight because of a school bus accident, but it's a decent little hospital. They'll take good care of you.''

''Where…?'' He swallowed to clear his thick voice, then tried again. ''Where is this hospital?''

''Edstown,'' she answered.

''Ed's town?'' he repeated blankly. ''Who's Ed?''

''I'm sorry, I thought you…it's Edstown,'' she said again ''Edstown, Arkansas.''

''Arkansas.'' He repeated the name of the state slowly, trying to make it mean something to him. ''How did I get here?''

''I found you lying in a ditch near my house. You had been severely beaten—perhaps left for dead. I called an ambulance and accompanied you here. Do you remember any of this?''

Actually, there were quite a few things he didn't remember—but he wasn't ready to get into that. Not with the word ''police'' still echoing hollowly in his mind.

She was studying him with a frown. ''Maybe I'd better go get a doctor….''

''No.'' He tried to hold up a hand to stop her, but both his arms seemed to be strapped down, the left wrist in a splint or bandage of some sort. ''Wait. Don't go yet.''

For some reason, he didn't want her to leave. He didn't want to lie here alone, hurting and fighting the confusion that was steadily threatening to overwhelm him. He was sure everything would come back to him once he'd had a chance to rest and recover for a few minutes. Considering the circumstances, it was no wonder he couldn't even remember his…

"Your name," the woman was saying. "You haven't even told me your name."

Tom? Dick? Harry? Nothing. Not a glimmer of recognition. How the hell could he forget his own name? he wondered in mounting frustration.

She seemed to go suddenly tense. "You *do* remember your name, don't you?"

He pictured her reaction if he admitted that his mind was achingly blank. She'd probably panic. She'd start calling doctors and nurses…maybe that chief of police she'd mentioned. The medical staff would rush in, poking and peering and treating him like some kind of freak, and who knew what the cop would believe. "Of course I remember my name."

She waited.

"Sam," he said, seizing the first moniker that came to him.

"Sam?" Her smooth brow wrinkled again. Obviously, his hasty answer hadn't satisfied her.

He groped for a surname. Nothing. His gaze skimmed the room as if searching for an answer. Bed. Chair. Floor. "Wall," he murmured. "Er…Wallace," he amended quickly.

He didn't know why he was so reluctant to admit the truth. Just tell her he couldn't for the life of him remember his name—or anything else that mattered. Actually, maybe *he* should be worried. He could be suffering brain damage. Something a doctor should look into immediately. Could be bleeding from the brain. God only knew what else. But something kept him quiet. He felt so stupid…he was sure it would all come back to him in a minute. He just needed a little time.

Whoever he was, he apparently believed in handling his own problems in his own way.

"Sam Wallace?" she repeated, a bit doubtfully.

Hell, why not? It would work until something better occurred to him. Like his real name. "Yeah. Sam Wallace. Who are you?"

"Serena Schaffer."

Serena. It suited her, he decided. "Thank you for rescuing me, Serena Schaffer," he said.

"I didn't do that much, but you're welcome. Now I really should get someone in here. The doctor will want to know you're awake...and Dan Meadows, our chief of police, wants to talk to you. Just to ask you a few questions about what happened to you."

The word *police* made him tense again. He wished he knew why. It was like...an instinct. Something inside him that told him to be very careful. At least until he remembered—

The door opened and a very large woman in a white uniform bustled in, shaking her head and muttering to herself. "What a night. I swear, if that Red Tucker says one more cross word to me, I'm going to snatch him bald-headed. We're taking care of all those kids the best we can, and he's out there... Oh, my, he's awake."

"Yes, we've been talking," Serena replied.

The nurse nodded. She leaned over the bed and peered into his eyes. "Headache?"

"Yeah," he said.

"He seems a little disoriented," Serena added, proving she hadn't been entirely fooled by his act.

The nurse didn't look surprised. "That's to be expected with the concussion. The doctor will be in soon, but they've got him running out there now."

He tried to nod, but went still when his head hammered in protest. "I'm not going anywhere."

She didn't smile. "How bad is the disorientation? Do you remember how you came to be here?"

According to Serena, he had been severely beaten. Left for dead in a ditch. "I know what happened."

"Do you remember the attack itself?"

It seemed safe enough to say, "Not much, I'm afraid."

"That's to be expected. Any other memory loss?"

He looked straight into her dark eyes. "No."

She seemed to believe him. Her pen hovered over the clipboard cradled in her left arm as she asked, "What's your name?"

"Sam Wallace."

"Middle initial?"

"None. Just Sam." The parents he'd just invented for himself weren't particularly creative. He wondered what his real parents were like. Were they even now looking for him, frantic with worry? Was he being a total idiot not to tell someone what was going on between his ears? The answer, of course, was yes. Still, he didn't change his mind.

"Birth date?"

As far as he could remember, he'd been born less than half an hour ago. He chose a date at random, finding it mildly curious that he could remember things like names and months and numbers, even though they held no personal meaning for him. "June twenty-second."

"Yeah? Today's the twentieth, so that means you've got a birthday coming up in a few days. What year were you born?"

Year? He wasn't even sure what year it was *now*.

He couldn't remember what he looked like, whether his hair was dark or light or gray—if he even had hair. He didn't feel old...but he didn't feel young, either.

Damn it, what was going on here? Why the *hell* couldn't he remember?

He groaned.

Serena stood and rested her hand on his shoulder, the gesture oddly protective. "He's obviously in pain, LuWanda. Isn't there anything you can do for him?"

LuWanda closed the clipboard. "I'll get the doctor."

He was grateful for the brief reprieve. He gave Serena a shamelessly pitiful look. "My head's killing me," he said.

She brushed a lank strand of hair off his forehead, her fingertips cool against his skin. So he did have hair. Nice to know.

"I'm sorry. Is there anything I can do for you? Someone I can call for you?"

He thought again of the family that could be searching for him. With a mental apology to them—if, indeed, they existed—he shook his head. "There isn't anyone to call, but thank you for offering."

What he really wanted right now was to be alone. A chance to think. To break through the mental barrier that was keeping him from his memories. He was certain that he could do so if he only had the time to work at it a bit...on his own, without disruptions. But as the door opened again and a short, squarely built older man he assumed to be the doctor strode briskly into the room, he knew it would be a while yet before he would be left alone. Now he had only to keep up his pretense until his mind cleared, which he fervently hoped it would do before he had to deal with the police. If the memories didn't return soon... Well, he would take this one step at a time.

Seeing the doctor, Serena smiled and stepped back. "I'll get out of the way now and let Dr. Frank take care of you. You're in good hands here, Sam."

Sam. The name sounded strange...but maybe just a little familiar? Was it possible that it really was his own? "You're leaving?"

Again, he found himself reluctant to see her go, perhaps because she was, for now, the first thing he remembered.

"Maybe we'll see each other again before you leave," she said lightly.

"I hope so," he murmured, and realized that he meant it. At the moment, she felt very much like his only friend.

The hospital was quiet, all the school bus passengers treated and released to the care of their relieved families. At the end of the hallway, Dan Meadows stood talking to an attractive young woman who was scribbling in a battered notebook. Serena could tell from the police chief's posture that he was rapidly growing impatient answering the reporter's questions. She moved to rescue him.

"As I said," she heard Dan saying in a flat, clipped voice, "no charges will be filed against the bus driver or anyone else until a full investigation of the accident has been conducted. Now I really don't know what else you want me to say, but—"

"What have I told you about hassling the local authorities, Lindsey?" Serena asked with a faint smile.

Her employee grinned with the irreverence Serena had come to expect from the youngest member of the

Evening Star staff. "You wouldn't deny me one of my favorite pastimes, would you?"

"For the sake of the newspaper's future dealings with the police department, I'm afraid I'm going to have to. Is there anything else you need for your article?"

"I've got everything I need about the bus accident," Lindsey answered. "But I hear we have another interesting story in Room Two Oh Five. Who's the mysterious stranger, Serena?"

"I'm waiting to hear that, myself," Dan said, giving Lindsey a repressive look. "Until we have all the facts, there's really nothing for you to write about him."

"Dan's right, Lindsey. All we know now is that he was found on Bullock Lake Road, suffering injuries from what appears to be a severe beating. I think you'll have to wait until tomorrow for further details. He's not strong enough to deal with the police and the press this evening."

"Is he awake yet?" Dan asked.

She nodded. "I talked to him for a few minutes. He said his name is Sam Wallace. I'm afraid that's pretty much the extent of what I learned about him. Dr. Frank's with him now."

"He refused to talk about what happened?" Dan frowned, as if that confirmed his suspicion that Sam Wallace had been involved in something shady.

Serena shook her head. "He didn't refuse. He's groggy, in pain. It seemed difficult for him to concentrate. He was quite pleasant, actually, just a bit confused. I'm not sure he even remembers what happened."

"He's claiming amnesia?" Dan's lip curled in open disbelief.

"No." Honestly, sometimes Dan took his official skepticism a bit too far. One would almost accuse him of being paranoid—if anyone had the nerve to do so to his face. "He's simply disoriented, Dan. I would imagine that's a fairly common reaction to a concussion."

He nodded reluctantly. "I'll try to talk to him when the doc's through with him. If he can identify his attackers, we'll have a better chance of finding them if we don't wait too long."

"He's in a lot of pain."

He gave her one of his rare smiles, though it didn't quite reach his glittering dark eyes. "Don't worry, Serena. I won't browbeat your stray. Just want to ask him some questions."

"So do I," Lindsey agreed.

Serena gave her a look. "Go file the school bus story. Everyone in town's going to want the details of that tomorrow."

Lindsey's expression implied that a mysterious wounded stranger was of as much interest to her as the mercifully minor school bus accident, but she had the discretion not to say so. She nodded. "I'll see you tomorrow, Serena. You, too, Chief. I'll be wanting details of your investigation into this guy's story, of course."

Dan glared after Lindsey as she sauntered into an elevator. "Have I ever mentioned that I really don't much like being questioned by your reporters all the time?"

"You've alluded to it a time or two," Serena replied. She knew Dan didn't mean anything personal against Lindsey, whom he'd known since she was a toddler. There were times she even suspected Dan was rather fond of Lindsey in his own gruff way—but he did not like reporters in general.

Dan had already turned his attention to the hospital room at the other end of the hall. "Okay, Sam Wallace," he murmured as if to himself. "Time to find out just who you are—an innocent crime victim, or someone we don't want in our town."

Serena had been wondering that herself. For some reason, she was having trouble picturing Sam Wallace—wounded or otherwise—as an innocent victim.

Chapter Two

Two hours later, Sam—the name he was still using for lack of a better one—was lying on his back in the hospital bed staring at the ten o'clock evening news on the TV mounted high on the wall across from his bed, hoping something would trigger the memories that had so far eluded him. He'd been straining to come up with even the foggiest detail, but the only result thus far was a pounding headache and a mounting frustration tinged with panic.

It was beginning to seem inevitable that he was going to have to admit the truth to someone—probably the cop who'd been in earlier, asking questions that Sam had deliberately answered as vaguely as possible. The chief had left with a promise that he would be back—or had it been a warning?

Sam wasn't at all sure Meadows had bought his story that he'd been passing through this area in search of work and had been mugged by a couple of guys who'd given him a lift. Claiming pain, fatigue and confusion, he hadn't given any details that would get anyone arrested, and Chief Meadows was not pleased with the sketchiness of the tale. Hell, for all Sam knew, it could be true. He just didn't remember any of it.

He cringed at the thought of saying aloud that he had lost his memory, that his mind was a blank, that he was utterly at the mercy of the staff of this tiny, apparently rural hospital. So far the characters he had encountered—with the exception of the cop—had been friendly, cheerful, laid-back and unpretentious. He had obviously landed in Smallville, U.S.A.—but from where?

He knew somehow he wasn't from around here; his speech patterns sounded different even to his own ears. Besides, he just didn't feel…Arkansan. Whatever the hell that meant.

But why was he here? Why had no one come forward to identify him? To ask about him? Was he really so alone that no one knew where he was? Was he as nameless and mysterious to everyone else as he was to himself at the moment?

He didn't like the idea that there was no one who cared whether he lived or died. Nor did he like lying in this bed wearing nothing but a backless hospital gown, a sheet so thin he could probably read a book through it, with a couple of bags of liquid dripping through a needle taped to his arm. Maybe if he could just see whatever he had been wearing when he'd been found, it would trigger his memory.

"What happened to my clothes?" he demanded of a thin, pale-skinned male who came in carrying a tray of vials and needles.

The man looked startled. He blinked almost lashless blue eyes. "Er, what clothes?"

"The ones I was wearing when I was brought in."

"I don't know, sir. I'll ask someone as soon as I get a blood sample."

"My blood's all been sampled. There's none left."

The technician looked as though he didn't know whether to smile. "Er..."

Sam sighed. "Hell. Just stick me and then find my clothes, will you?"

He was beginning to lose patience with all of this. The hospital, its staff—and his own stubbornly closed mind.

He was informed a short while later that he hadn't been carrying a wallet, at least not that anyone from the hospital staff had found. There had been, he was assured, nothing in the pockets of his jeans or shirt. While his lack of personal items backed up his story of having been robbed, it gave him no clue as to his identity.

"Damn," he growled as soon as he was alone again. Why couldn't he remember? What was wrong with him?

Another nurse came in, this one tall and bony. "I'm Lydia, your nurse for this shift. How are you feeling?"

He eyed her warily. "That depends. What are you planning to poke into me?"

She smiled and held up a thermometer. "Only this. Pain free, I assure you."

He reluctantly opened his mouth.

"Oh, and I have to ask you some questions," she added, opening a clipboard and snapping a ballpoint. "LuWanda never finished filling out these papers and admissions is having a hissy fit."

He nearly swallowed the thermometer. "Mmph."

"Hold on a second." She waited until the electronic thermometer beeped, then pulled it out and glanced at it. "Normal."

He wouldn't have advised her to bet money on that.

"Now, about this form. All we've got so far is your name, Sam Wallace, and the month and day of your birth. June twenty-second. Correct so far?"

"Uh, yeah."

"What year were you born, Mr. Wallace?"

He managed a smile. "How old do I look?"

She rolled her eyes. "He wants to play games," she murmured. "Okay, I'm supposed to humor the patient. You look..." She eyed him consideringly while he held his breath. "Thirty-three?"

"Thirty-one," he corrected with an exaggerated grimace. It sounded like a nice age. Not too young, not too old.

"So you were born in nineteen..." Her voice trailed off as she scribbled numbers on her form.

"Address?"

"I'm, um, between addresses right now. Between jobs, too," he added to answer her next question.

"Do you have insurance?"

Lady, I don't even have a name. "No."

"Next of kin?"

He closed his eyes. "None."

"Are you in pain?"

"Just a mother of a headache."

"I'm sorry. Only a few more questions. Are you allergic to any medications?"

He was tired. So damned tired. He should tell her the truth. *I can't remember. There's nothing between*

*my ears but dead air. Call in your experts, lady. One
genuine freak, here for their viewing pleasure.*

He couldn't do it. Maybe he'd tell someone tomorrow. Or maybe by then it wouldn't be necessary.

"No," he murmured. "I'm not allergic to anything." And it would serve him right if they injected him with something and he died a horrible, painful death from an allergic reaction.

She asked him other questions about his medical history. Keeping his eyes closed, he made up answers in a lethargic monotone.

*You're an idiot, Sam. Or whoever the hell you are.
A coward. A fool. A liar. A jerk. Tell the lady the truth.*

But still he lied. For he, himself, was afraid of the truth.

He heard her close the cover of the clipboard. "All right," she said. "That's enough for now."

Sam let out a long, ragged breath when he was finally alone again. He was so fatigued he could hardly move, both mentally and physically exhausted. Every inch of him ached. He needed rest. He wanted out of this place. He hadn't a clue where he would go when he left.

He didn't even know what he looked like, but there were a few things he'd learned about himself during the past couple of hours. He had more pride than was good for him, he didn't like admitting weakness or vulnerability and he utterly hated being at the mercy of others.

All those traits felt familiar to him. Felt right. So who the hell was he? And why couldn't he remember?

He really was a nice-looking man beneath the bruises. Even flat on his back in a hospital bed, there was a sort of…well, grace to him, Serena mused the next morning, studying Sam from the chair beside the bed. His lips were slightly parted, and he wheezed a little when he breathed—a result of the blows he'd taken to his chest. His lashes were long against his scraped cheeks, oddly dark in contrast to his golden hair. Those thick curling lashes were the only softening feature on his firmly carved face.

She thought of the sketchy history he'd given Dan. He'd implied that he was a rootless drifter, rambling from place to place, supporting himself with temporary jobs. No permanent home, no family. Looking again at his beautifully shaped hands, marred only by the abrasions across his knuckles, she wondered what the odds were that those temporary jobs had involved sitting behind desks crunching numbers. She found it hard to believe those rather elegant hands had ever wielded a shovel or a sledge hammer. And if his clean oval nails hadn't been professionally manicured recently, she'd kiss her sister's dog—right on his slobbery mouth.

Raising her gaze from the man's hands to his face, she was momentarily disconcerted to find his brilliant blue eyes open and trained unblinkingly on her. "Oh. Good morning."

"Serena."

He said her name as if it was important that he had remembered it. She nodded. "Serena Schaffer."

"You're the one who found me."

"Yes. How are you feeling?"

"Tired. Have you ever tried to sleep in a hospital?"

"No. I've never been hospitalized."

"I don't recommend it. Every few minutes someone

comes in to draw blood, take your blood pressure and temperature and listen through a stethoscope that feels like it's stored in a freezer. They're obsessed with my bodily fluids—intake and output. Every time I try to move into a more comfortable position, this damned IV pump starts beeping, nagging at me to be still.'' To demonstrate, he bent his right arm, kinking the thin tube that ran from the IV pump to the needle taped into the back of his hand. A moment later the pump began to beep, and darned if it didn't sound petulant. Sam sighed and straightened his arm. The machine went silent.

Serena had waited patiently through his litany of complaints. ''Does it feel better to have that off your chest?''

His bruised mouth quirked. ''A bit.''

''Then I'm glad I was here to listen.''

''I guess I unloaded on you because you're the first person to come into this room in hours who wasn't carrying a needle.''

''Are you sure there isn't someone I can call for you? A friend or family member who could be with you while you recover?''

''There really isn't anyone I want notified right now. But thanks for offering.''

She wouldn't want to be so alone in a hospital. She knew if anything happened to her, she would have legions of family and friends around her, giving her sympathy and support. She felt sorry for anyone who didn't have that emotional base to draw strength from.

He must have read her expression. ''I'm fine,'' he assured her. ''I'll just be glad to get out of here.''

''Where will you go then?''

The corners of his mouth tightened. She couldn't

tell if he was annoyed with her questioning or unhappy with the answer. Was it true that he had no place to go? No one to turn to? Serena would hate to find herself in that position.

When it became obvious that he had no answer for her, she changed the subject. "I talked to Chief Meadows earlier. He said he hasn't made any headway in finding the two men who robbed and beat you. There's been no sign of that pieced-together pickup truck you described."

"I'm not surprised. I don't think they were from around here. Probably just passing through the area, looking for trouble."

"Like you?" she asked in a murmur.

He met her eyes without blinking. "I wasn't looking for trouble. Unfortunately, it found me, anyway."

She knew that feeling. She hadn't been looking for trouble when she'd found Sam Wallace in that ditch, either. But she *had* found him—well, her sister's dog did—and now, for some stupid reason, she felt rather responsible for him.

The sounds of the hospital drifted in through the door she'd left partially open. Nurses talked, equipment beeped, someone coughed, someone else cried. Illness seemed to creep through the hallways like a malicious spirit, constantly trying to outsmart the few overworked doctors in this small, outdated and underfunded institution. The staff did the best they could with what they had, but most folks in these parts went elsewhere for serious medical attention, into bigger towns with more financial advantages. Serena hoped her stranger was getting the care he needed here. Head injuries were so unpredictable.

LuWanda, the heavyset nurse who'd taken care of Sam when he'd arrived, marched in. "Time to take your vitals, Mr. Wallace."

He scowled. "You can just damned well leave my vitals alone."

LuWanda laughed as though he'd made a light-hearted jest. "Don't worry, I won't touch anything I haven't touched before. Oh, and I want to get a pulse ox reading. The doc's still concerned about those blows you took to the chest. Have to make sure you're getting plenty of oxygen."

He gave Serena a look as the nurse clipped something around his right index finger. "Pulse ox," he murmured.

She stood. "Whatever that is, I hope yours is good."

"Ninety-nine percent," the nurse announced when something chirped. "Better than mine—I smoked for twenty years. Guess you're not a smoker, huh, Mr. Wallace?"

"Guess not," he answered vaguely.

Serena took a step closer to the bed. "I have to go. Is there anything I can get for you, Sam? Books, magazines, personal items?"

"No, thank you. I'm fine."

Definitely the independent sort, she thought. He had nothing to his name but a backless hospital gown and he still didn't ask for anything. A very intriguing man, this Sam Wallace—whoever he was.

"Well, then—I'll see you later." She moved toward the door. She had no doubt that she would be back. Something about the lonely, slightly confused expression in his bright blue eyes kept pulling her here.

Was she being a complete fool to let herself get involved with him, even on this temporary and casual basis?

"Well? What did you find out about him?" Petite, red-haired, green-eyed Lindsey Gray pounced the moment Serena walked into the *Evening Star* offices. "You went to see him at the hospital again, didn't you? Did you talk to him? Did you learn more details about what happened to him?"

"Lindsey, take a breath or something," Serena ordered, shaking her head in exasperation. "Geez, you'd think we'd never seen a stranger in this town before."

"We haven't very often. And never quite like this— so what did you find out?"

Tucking a strand of hair behind her ear, Serena gave a little shrug. "You've heard as much as I have. He said he was hitching through this area looking for temporary work when two men in a patched-together pickup truck gave him a ride, robbed him, beat him up and left him for dead in that ditch. He can't describe the men very well because he has very little memory of the beating—a slight memory loss due to the concussion, which the doctor said is normal."

"Where's he from? What's his story?"

"I don't know. He didn't say, and I didn't ask many questions. He's in a lot of discomfort, Lindsey. He isn't up to being interviewed."

Lindsey pouted. She was the only twenty-five-year-old woman Serena knew who could actually pout and get away with it.

To her disgust, Lindsey was destined to be thought of as cute, when what she really wanted to be was sharp and sophisticated. After obtaining a degree in journalism, she had gone to work for a newspaper in Little Rock for a couple of years before moving back to her little hometown to be close to her father, who was in ill health. She'd taken a significant pay cut to work for the *Evening Star,* but she took the job very seriously, attacking it with the same dedication she'd have given a position with the *Washington Post* or *New York Times.*

Sometimes Serena thought Lindsey took her job *too* seriously. She was constantly on the lookout for the "big story"— and the truth was, there just weren't that many big stories in Edstown. With the exception of a recent rash of burglaries, not much happened around these parts. She mercilessly hounded the mayor and poor Chief Meadows, both of whom held a deep distrust of reporters and an ingrained aversion to any bad press about their town. But there was no doubt that the newspaper had been better since Lindsey arrived.

Speaking of which, Serena glanced around the unarguably shabby offices, which were quiet and deserted now that the evening edition had been printed and delivered. She knew some people were born with ink in their veins, that the smell of newsprint and the sounds of press machines gave them an almost sexual thrill. Serena looked around and saw only clutter and chaos.

She had never wanted to own her great-grandfather's newspaper. That had been the destiny of her older sister, Kara. Serena was a lawyer, not a newshound, and she would just as soon have kept it that way. Unfortunately, there'd been no one else to take over after their father died last year, and three months later Kara left town with a wanna-be country music star, leaving Serena with Kara's stupid dog and full responsibility for Great-granddad's newspaper. Her first impulse had been to sell, but the very idea had distressed her mother so much that Serena had reluctantly agreed to give it a shot.

"Where's Marvin?" she asked, glancing at the managing editor's empty office. "He and I were supposed to discuss last month's ad revenues this evening."

Lindsey rolled her eyes. "Where do you *think* he is? He decided to pop over to Gaylord's for a 'quick nip' before your meeting. That was two hours ago."

There would be no discussing anything with Marvin tonight, Serena thought with a grimace. The aging editor—a longtime crony of her late grandfather's—had been spending more and more time at Gaylord's since his wife died two years ago. Marvin was tired and lonely and burned out, resistant to modern technology, nostalgic for the old days, but he didn't want to retire. He'd said he would have no reason at all to get out of bed if he didn't have a job to go to. As much as she truly hated the very thought, Serena was beginning to believe that she was going to have to pressure Marvin into retirement. It broke her heart, but it was rapidly becoming necessary.

Damn it, Kara, this should be your job.

Pushing a hand through her hair, she sighed heavily. "I'll try to catch him tomorrow, I guess. Are you finished for the night?"

Lindsey shook her head and hoisted her oversize macramé bag onto her shoulder. "I'm going to the town council meeting. I'd better get moving, it starts in ten minutes."

"I thought Riley was covering the council meeting tonight."

"He is. I'm just going out of curiosity. Maybe I'll have a chance to corner Dan after the meeting to ask what he's found out about the men who mugged your stranger."

"He isn't *my* stranger," Serena protested, though she was uncomfortably aware she'd fallen into the habit of thinking of him that way.

Lindsey waved a hand dismissively. "I'd just like to know exactly what Dan has done. What he's found out—about the muggers *or* the victim. And what he's going to do tomorrow."

"You know how Dan hates it when you badger him about the way he does his job."

Lindsey broke into a bright, impish smile—the one that transformed her face from cute to strikingly attractive. "I know. Why do you think I keep doing it?"

Though she would never mention it, Serena had long suspected that Lindsey carried a secret torch for the police chief. If it was true, Lindsey's case seemed pretty hopeless. Dan was ten years her senior and a lifelong friend of Lindsey's older brother. He tended to regard Lindsey as his own kid sister—when he didn't see her as an annoying member of the press. Dan had also been through a divorce so ugly and bitter the townspeople were still talking about it two years later. He had said he was in no hurry to get seriously involved with anyone again. If ever.

All in all, it seemed a distinctly unlikely match. But maybe she was wrong about Lindsey's feelings. Maybe Lindsey just enjoyed watching Dan foam at the mouth while she buzzed around him with her stubbornly persistent questions.

"Okay, go ask your questions," Serena said with a

quick laugh. "And, Lindsey, if you find out anything, let me know, okay?"

Lindsey sketched an impudent salute. "You got it, boss."

Twenty-four hours. The man who had dubbed himself Sam Wallace shifted restlessly in the hospital bed, tried to lift his left hand to his face, winced, then raised his right hand instead. The IV pump bleated at him to straighten his arm. He cursed it beneath his breath but laid his arm down just to shut it up.

It had been just over twenty-four hours since Serena found him in that ditch. And his head was still as empty as the tiny closet provided for the belongings he hadn't brought with him.

Frustration was beginning to eat at him. How could he remember so many trivial details—the president of the United States, the taste of chocolate ice cream, the irritation of too-starched shirts—yet not remember his own damned name? How could he recall the name of every bloodthirsty nurse he'd encountered since he'd arrived in this place and not remember his own mother?

Maybe he should just give in and confess the truth to the next person who entered that door. Let 'em poke him and probe him, X-ray his brain and find the holes there, bring in the shrinks and neurologists and whoever else they wanted to study him like a strange bug on a microscope slide. Amnesia, they would call it, and then they would look at him like he was some sort of freak or faker, because true amnesia was damned rare. He remembered that fact. He didn't know how.

There was a quick rap on the door and then the night nurse entered. ''You doing okay, Mr. Wallace?''

''Just peachy,'' he drawled. He knew he wouldn't be spilling the truth tonight. Maybe tomorrow, if the condition hadn't already corrected itself by then. Or maybe he'd be dead by morning, felled by obstinacy and pride. At the moment, he was finding it real hard to care.

Chapter Three

"The poor man. We have to do something to help him."

Serena wasn't at all surprised by her mother's words. Marjorie Schaffer was an obsessive do-gooder. She belonged to every charitable organization in the area, had been president of most of them, had chaired every community outreach committee at her church, was still active in PTA more than ten years after her youngest daughter finished high school and would willingly give the clothes off her back to help someone in need. She had just decided that Sam Wallace fit that description.

"We have to be careful, Mother. We don't really know anything about this guy," Serena said, shaking a finger warningly at her mother. Dressed in baggy pajamas, she sat at the table in the kitchen, a cup of tea in front of her and her sister's dog snoring at her feet. Her mother sat across the table in a matched peignoir set, her hair and makeup so perfect she looked as though she was posing for a photograph in a women's magazine.

Marjorie didn't seem at all concerned about Serena's admonition. "You've spoken with him twice. You said he seemed quite pleasant."

"Right. And Ted Bundy was known for his charm," Serena retorted. "Really, Mother, this Sam Wallace could be a con man or a criminal, for all we know. It doesn't make sense that he was just drifting through this area without a car or a destination. He hasn't divulged anything about who he really is or where he's from."

"Obviously, he's a man who's down on his luck and in need of compassion. We'll have to see what we can do to help him."

Serena grimaced. "At least wait until Dan finishes his investigation before you get involved, will you? As suspicious as Dan is of outsiders, he'll make it a point to find out if there's any reason for us to be wary of Mr. Wallace."

Marjorie murmured something noncommittal, then changed the subject before Serena could nag a promise from her. "Did I mention that Kara called while you were at work today?"

That too-casual announcement made Serena sit up straighter. "She did? How is she? Has she come to her senses? Is she coming home to take her place at the paper and reclaim this idiot mutt of hers?"

Marjorie's laugh was tinged with just a hint of wistfulness. "I'm afraid not. She is still desperately in love with Pierce and determined to help him become a country music star. She's waiting tables at a little nightclub outside of Nashville while he sings there three nights a week hoping to be discovered."

Serena groaned. She honestly wondered if her older sister had lost her mind. Kara had always been as responsible and dependable as Serena, outwardly content to settle in Edstown and take over the family-owned newspaper. She'd been engaged briefly during her senior year of college, but that hadn't worked out, and she'd seemed in no rush to get involved again.

Marjorie had often fretted that neither of her daughters was anxious to marry and start families, both focused more on establishing their careers and their independence than finding the right men. "Too picky," she had called them, reminding them often that there weren't many single males to choose from in this area and advising them to grab a couple before they were all gone.

Eight months ago, thirty-one-year-old Kara had met twenty-six-year-old Pierce Vanness during a girls' night out at a bar in a neighboring town. Pierce had been the entertainment that evening, singing with a local band. Like a star-struck groupie, Kara had approached him between sets—and the rest was history. Kara had convinced Pierce to give up his day job working in his father's shoe store and head for Nashville in search of stardom. She'd named herself his business manager—which seemed to involve supporting him while he pursued his dream.

Serena just couldn't understand it.

Marjorie spent the next twenty minutes filling Serena in on all the details of Kara's call. It occurred to Serena only after she'd gone up to bed that Marjorie had never promised to stay away from Sam Wallace until after Dan had thoroughly investigated him.

* * *

Sam sat in a chair in his hospital room, gazing out the window at the uninspiring view of the parking lot. The doctor had said it would be good for him to get out of bed, that it would help him build up his strength. Sam was more than ready for that, but he saw no evidence of it yet. His limbs were still as rubbery as a jellyfish. He didn't want to believe that was a normal condition for him.

The ever-present IV pump stood on its wheeled stand beside his chair, chugging liquids into him through the needle still taped into the back of his hand. He was idly considering using the heavy metal stand to break the window and escape this place when someone tapped on his door and then pushed it open. Expecting one of his nurses, he was a bit surprised when his caller turned out to be a comfortably rounded woman in her mid-fifties with beauty-parlor curls lacquered into her salt-and-pepper hair and soft blue eyes behind plastic-framed glasses. She wore a pale green knit pantsuit and she carried a large black purse in one small hand.

"Mr. Wallace?" she asked.

Without confirming the name, he responded, "What can I do for you?"

She bustled into the room. As far as he could remember, he'd never actually seen anyone bustle before, but it was the only word that seemed to describe this woman's quick, almost fluttery steps. "Actually, I'm here to find out what I can do for *you*. I'm Marjorie Schaffer."

Shrink? Social worker? Had someone figured out his problem already? Acutely aware of his scratched bare legs sticking out from beneath the gown and paper-thin robe the hospital had provided, Sam cleared his throat. "Um—yes?"

"I'm Serena's mother. She told me all about you."

Relaxing a little, he murmured, "Did she?" It must not have been much of a conversation, considering how little there was to tell about him at this point.

Marjorie Schaffer bobbed her head. "She said you were passing through looking for work when two evil men robbed you and beat you up. I'm so sorry, Mr. Wallace. I hate to think anyone around here would do such a terrible thing."

Just what he needed to flood him with guilt—this sweet little woman apologizing for a crime he'd concocted from thin air. He tugged his robe over his bare knees, trying to decide what to say in response.

She didn't give him a chance to speak, but sank almost royally into the other chair and gazed at him kindly. "You have no family to turn to in your time of need, Mr. Wallace?"

"Um...no. No close family, anyway."

"I'm so sorry. I've lost both my parents, as well as my husband. It's very difficult to be left so alone, isn't it? I don't know what I would do without my daughters."

"Serena has a sister?"

"An older sister, Kara. She's living in Nashville, Tennessee, now. She calls often, though. And she knows she's always welcome to come home—and that Serena and I would both be there immediately if she needs us."

Because she seemed to expect a comment, he said, "You're very fortunate to have each other."

Was there someone even now frantically searching for *him?* Ready and willing to offer him the type of comfort and support Marjorie Schaffer had just described? Someone who loved him enough to drop everything to come to him? He strained to remember, but the only result was a throbbing headache and a hollow feeling in his chest. If he had a loving family somewhere, they were as lost to him now as his real name.

The memories would come back when his injuries healed, he assured himself. And then he would offer a sincere apology to anyone who might have suffered because of his unplanned absence. But if there *was* someone who loved him—someone he loved in return—wouldn't he sense it? Somehow?

"Mr. Wallace?" Marjorie broke into his torturous self-questioning, her soft face creased with concern as she leaned toward him. "Are you in pain?"

He immediately cleared his expression. "Just a headache."

"Poor dear." She patted his braced left hand, exactly as if he were a wounded six-year-old. "Should I call a nurse?"

Reacting instinctively to her tone, he answered, "No, ma'am. That isn't necessary."

"You're sure?"

"Yes, thank you. Someone will be in soon enough."

She sat back with a sympathetic smile. "If you're anything like my late husband, you hate being in the hospital. He couldn't abide the loss of privacy and dignity, even for his own good."

That was a sentiment Sam heartily shared. "The doctor told me this morning that I'll probably be released tomorrow. Most likely before noon."

"So soon?"

Having seen himself in the bathroom mirror, he understood her surprise. The colorful scrapes and bruises that covered most of his exposed skin looked every bit as bad as they felt. He didn't know whether it was those bruises or the amnesia that had made his face look so much like a stranger to him. But the injuries weren't life-threatening, and the hospital administrators were probably growing a bit nervous about his lack of insurance. There was little more that could be done for him here. Time and patience were the best medicines for him now.

He just wished he knew where the hell he would go when he was ushered, barefoot and penniless, out of this place. If his memory had not returned by that point, he would be forced to admit the truth to someone. What else could he do?

"Where will you go when you leave here?" Marjorie asked, as if she'd somehow read his thoughts.

"I'm not sure." He kept his tone deliberately nonchalant. "I guess I'll play that by ear."

"What sort of work were you hoping to find before those awful men attacked you?"

Again, he didn't know quite how to answer her. It was harder, for some reason, to lie to this kind-eyed woman than it had been with the others. Yet something deep inside him refused to let the truth come out. Pride? Fear? He didn't know what instinct held him back, what repercussions he feared most, but he was no more willing to confess his amnesia now than he had been before.

"As long as it's legal, I'm not particularly selective about the jobs I take," he said, bluffing.

"What about waiting tables? Is that a job you would consider?"

"Waiting tables?" He had a vague image of himself sitting in a dimly lit restaurant while white-coated servers set plates of food in front of him. Obviously a glimmer of memory—but where was that restaurant? And who had been sitting on the other side of the table for two he'd envisioned? "I can wait tables."

She nodded, looking curiously satisfied. "Good. If you're interested, I have a job for you. You can start as soon as you've recovered sufficiently to be on your feet for several hours."

"You, uh, have a job for me?"

"Yes. I own a little diner downtown. The Rainbow Café. We're open Monday through Saturday for breakfast and lunch, and we do a brisk business on weekdays. I've just lost two employees. You can work for me when you're released—or as soon as you're physically able, if you need a few days to recover first."

Sam blinked a couple of times. "Um…a diner?" He couldn't seem to stop foolishly parroting her.

She nodded brusquely. "I can't pay you a lot, of course, but you're in no shape to work at construction or other more physically challenging jobs. You can work for me at least until you recover all your strength, which might take a few weeks."

"Why are you offering this, Mrs. Schaffer?" He was pretty sure this generous offer was unusual from a complete stranger.

Her smile was angelic. "Because I need your help, Mr. Wallace. And because you need mine. That seems like a fair trade, doesn't it?"

Surely his memory would return by tomorrow. Maybe he would remember that he did, indeed, have insurance—or a couple of million dollars set aside for emergencies. But just in case... "Thank you. I accept your offer."

She nodded as if there'd never been any doubt. "You'll need a place to stay, of course."

"I'm sure I can—"

"I have a place you can use until you get something more permanent. It's a little one-bedroom guest house my late husband built for my mother a few years before she passed away. It's completely separate from the house Serena and I share, so you would have your privacy. You're welcome to stay there rent-free while you're working to pay off your medical bills. If you want to stay longer than that, we can discuss rent then."

"You're being very kind." Scary-kind, actually. Did normal people really do things like this?

She beamed at him. "I've been accused of making snap judgments, but I'm almost always correct in my instincts about people. I know you're a good man, Sam. You just need a little help right now."

He was humbled by her blind faith in him. He hoped she was right. He wanted to believe he was one of the good guys, but for all he knew, he could be a bum or a con man. If the latter was true, he was pulling a hell of a scam this time. He'd even managed to fool himself.

Marjorie stood. "That's all settled, then. I'm sure my daughter will be by to visit you later. You let her know if you need anything, you hear? We'll take care of it."

"Mrs. Schaffer—" He wanted to stand, but that didn't seem like a very good idea just then, since he would probably fall flat on his face. "Are you sure about all this? As touched as I am by your faith in me, we both know I'm still very much a stranger to you. I would hate to disappoint you."

She patted his head—exactly as though he were that sick child in need of reassurance, he couldn't help thinking again. "My husband's favorite quote was the one that says there are no strangers, only friends we haven't met yet. Now that we've met, I'd like to think we'll become friends, Sam. I'll see you soon."

Some time later he was still staring at the door through which she had disappeared, and still utterly bemused by her unexpected offers. Just what kind of place had he landed in, anyway? Very little so far seemed real to him.

The name *Brigadoon* flitted through his mind, and he had a vague idea that it was a fictional town with strange, magical properties. From a book he'd read, perhaps, or a film he'd seen—he couldn't quite remember. He did remember that the people who lived there could never escape.

Was Edstown, Arkansas, his own personal Brigadoon?

Later that day, Serena paused in the doorway of the hospital room in a very uncertain frame of mind. Sam was lying in his bed, staring at the television mounted high on the wall. The TV was tuned to a cable news network, and he was watching as intently as though he would be tested on the subject matter later that evening. His expression was similar to the one that had tugged at her heartstrings before. The one that looked...lost.

"Mr. Wallace?"

He didn't quite start, but she'd obviously taken him

by surprise. He turned his head to look at her, then offered a faint smile of greeting. "Ms. Schaffer."

"You called me Serena before," she reminded him, stepping farther into the room.

"And you called me Sam before."

"Yes." She perched on the edge of the straight-backed visitor's chair beside his bed. "I heard you met my mother today."

"Yes. She's quite...unusual. A delightful woman."

"Both adjectives are correct," she assured him. "She *is* delightful...and most definitely unusual."

"Is she always so trusting of strangers?"

Watching his face closely, Serena shook her head. "She isn't particularly gullible, if that's what you're asking—though I can see why you might think she is. She really is a shrewd judge of character, and a sharp businesswoman. She simply makes her decisions about people very quickly."

"And she's never been swindled by anyone she trusted so quickly?"

"Not as far as I know. At least, not in any significant way."

He shook his head in obvious amazement. "That's hard to believe. Did she tell you she offered me a job? And a place to live?"

She had, actually—and Serena's first response had been dismay. "Have you lost your mind?" she had asked her mother. "You've invited a total stranger to live in our own backyard?"

"Serena, he's a very nice man who needs our help," Marjorie had answered calmly. "What kind of people would we be if we turned our backs on someone in that poor man's circumstances?"

"And what will happen to us if he *isn't* a very nice man?"

Marjorie had waved off the question with typical confidence in her own judgment, leaving Serena to do the worrying.

"My mother has a soft heart and a generous nature," Serena said to Sam. "I would hate for anyone to try to take advantage of those traits."

"If that's a not-so-veiled warning, I received it loud and clear."

She kept her smile cool. "I hope so."

"I take it you don't share your mother's predilection for snap judgments."

"I tend to be a bit more cautious about giving my trust."

He was watching her now as closely as she'd studied him earlier. "That's very wise of you."

"The truth is, I'm not as good as my mother at reading people. I've learned to be more careful."

"Personal experience being burned?"

"Once or twice." She quickly changed the subject. "So you're going to work in the diner. Do you have training for waiting tables?"

He shrugged. "How hard can it be?"

She couldn't help smiling at that. She would love to be around to watch his first encounter with her mother's busy lunch crowd, all of them in a hurry to eat and return to their jobs. "Mom said you're being released tomorrow. Do you know what time?"

"Sometime tomorrow morning. Before noon, they said."

"I'll be here to pick you up. Is there anything you need me to bring in the morning?"

His eyebrows rose. "You understand that your

mother has offered to let me stay in your guest house?''

"Yes, I know. She's probably dusting and freshening it as we speak."

"And you have no objections to this arrangement?"

"I suppose not. After all, Mother already offered."

"And you claim that *she* is the trusting one in the family?"

Serena wrinkled her nose at him, amused by his expression. "I don't have to completely trust you to give you a hand in the morning. Not that I *don't* trust you, of course," she added quickly, in case he'd taken offense. "What I meant to say is—"

He laughed. The sound was so unexpected—and so pleasant—that it silenced her babbling. "I know what you meant," he assured her. "And there's no need to apologize. I appreciate your help. I hope I can find a way to repay you and your mother someday for the kindness you've shown me."

Somewhat stiffly, she murmured, "I wasn't apologizing."

"Good."

A young woman in teddy-bear-print scrubs carried a covered tray into the room. "Dinner, Mr. Wallace."

He eyed the tray without enthusiasm. "I don't suppose you've got a thick steak under there? Or maybe lasagna?"

With an apologetic smile, she set the tray on the wheeled bed table. "I'm afraid not. It's macaroni and cheese with English peas and Jell-O."

The look Sam gave Serena almost made her laugh. It was quite clear that he wasn't looking forward to his dinner.

"There's a corn bread muffin to go with it," the

young woman said almost anxiously, as if eager to please him. "I've heard the corn bread is pretty good."

Displaying a smoothness that immediately set off Serena's alarms, Sam gave the woman a near-blinding smile. "I'm sure I'll enjoy it, then. Thank you."

"You're welcome." She almost stammered, and she was blushing when she hurried out of the room.

Serena doubted that this little hospital had seen many patients like golden-haired, blue-eyed, wicked-dimpled Sam Wallace. She'd heard gossip that the nurses had all but competed with each other to take his vital signs. LuWanda had told her in the hallway earlier that he was one of the nicest young men she'd ever taken care of. "So funny and polite," she'd raved. "It's such a shame about his circumstances. Something terrible must have happened to cause such a smart, obviously well-educated man to end up without a home or a job. No one to turn to in his time of need."

"Maybe he's just a loner," Serena had suggested. "Someone who can't stay in one place for very long. One of those guys who's incapable of forming lasting attachments."

"I don't think so," LuWanda had murmured thoughtfully. "Have you seen the look in his eyes? Something tragic happened to him—maybe the death of someone he loved deeply or something awful like that. He's running from a broken heart or tragic memories. I'd bet my next week's salary on it."

Remembering those fanciful words, Serena studied Sam's eyes. Once again the first adjective that came to her mind when she tried to identify his expression was "lost." She wasn't sure if Sam Wallace was running away from something or looking for something, but he was obviously not a happy man. But, oh, could he turn on the charm.

Before he could wonder why she was just sitting there staring at him, Serena stood. "I'll leave you to your delicious dinner."

"Gee, thanks."

She chuckled at his unenthusiastic response. "I'll see you in the morning, Sam."

She was aware that he watched her leave—as if he was reluctant to see her go. The poor guy must really be lonely, she thought—and then realized in annoyed exasperation that she was beginning to sound just like her mother. Both of them had darned well better be careful—just in case Sam Wallace wasn't as charming as he appeared.

Chapter Four

By ten the next morning, Sam was free to go. The IV had been removed and he'd been given a list of instructions and a few painkillers, in case he needed them. The only thing he didn't have was clothes. He was still wearing the backless cotton hospital gown. The shirt and pants he'd worn when he'd been brought in had been cut away, he was apologetically informed. Someone would try to find him a pair of pajamas to leave in.

He was working up to a pretty good case of self-pity when Serena came into his room, her arms filled with blue plastic discount store bags. "I brought you some clothes," she said without preamble. "They aren't exactly designer label, and I had to guess at sizes, but they should do until you can replace your own things."

He eyed the pile of bags she had dumped unceremoniously on the foot of the bed. "You bought me clothes?"

She shrugged, obviously determined not to make a big deal of it. "Just a few things. Almost all of it was on sale. I picked up two pairs of shoes in different sizes. I hope one of them fits. I'll take the other pair back for a refund."

He was oddly touched by her actions, and by her painfully self-conscious expression. "Thank you."

She avoided his eyes. "I'll go have a cup of coffee or something while you get dressed."

"I won't take long. I'm more than ready to get out of this place."

He'd been half afraid Dr. Purtle—the man everyone referred to as Dr. Frank—was going to change his mind about the release. Sam wasn't sure what he'd done wrong during the exam that morning, but Dr. Frank hadn't seemed quite satisfied with the results. He'd asked repeatedly if Sam was experiencing a headache—which he wasn't—and if he was sure he was seeing clearly—which he was. And then he'd asked if Sam was experiencing any loss of memory other than about the attack itself, which was natural. Sam had looked the kindly, concerned older man straight in the eye and lied through his teeth.

"No memory gaps, Doc," he had said. And it hadn't been a real lie, he reflected bitterly. There were no gaps in his memory. There was no memory at all. Not a clue who he'd been or what he'd done prior to waking up in this hospital with Serena Schaffer sitting beside his bed.

He didn't know if the amnesia was a sign of a physical problem or an emotional one—maybe he just didn't *want* to remember his past—but it was real.

Whether he was brain damaged or a candidate for a psych ward, no amount of effort on his part had brought forth a single detail about his life. He probably *did* belong on a psych ward. What kind of nutcase would let himself be released from a hospital without admitting to anyone that there was still something seriously wrong with him?

To distract himself from a question that had no rational answer, he dug in the bags Serena had carried in. He found underwear, T-shirts and tube socks. Two pairs of classic styled jeans, a brown leather belt and three T-shirts in assorted colors. Two button-up shirts—one white, one blue denim. A package of disposable razors, a can of shaving cream, toothbrush, toothpaste and a comb—things the hospital had provided for him, but thoughtful additions on Serena's part. And the two pairs of sneakers she'd mentioned—size ten and eleven. For all he knew, he wore an eight or fourteen—his shoe size was as lost to him as his real name.

Fifteen minutes later he had to acknowledge that Serena had a good eye for sizes. He wore the denim shirt with a pair of jeans and the size-eleven shoes. The thirty-four-inch-waist jeans were a little loose, but he cinched the belt to make up for it. The shirt fit perfectly.

He was frowning at the bruise the IV needle had left on his hand when Serena tapped on the door and then entered. She appraised his appearance with one quick, comprehensive glance. "Looks like my guesses were close."

"Everything fits fine. You can return the size-ten shoes. I'll pay you back for everything as soon as I can."

"There's no rush," she assured him, looking uncomfortable again. "You'll need to pay your medical bills first. Actually, you could consider the clothes a birthday present."

"A birthday present?" he repeated blankly.

She smiled. "Today's the twenty-second. Had you forgotten?"

June twenty-second. The day he'd selected at random when the nurse had asked for his date of birth. At the time, he hadn't even known it *was* June. He wished now he'd chosen a date in December. "I'll pay you back for the clothes," he said, and he tried to make it clear that he didn't want any further argument about it.

Serena only shrugged and turned toward the remaining packages. "I should have thought to include a duffel bag or something. I guess these bags will have to do for now. I'll tell LuWanda we're ready to go. I think you have to leave in a wheelchair."

"I think not." The very suggestion made his lip curl.

Eyeing his expression, Serena said hastily, "I'm sure they'll let you walk, if you prefer."

Fortunately, LuWanda didn't try to insist on a wheelchair. "You take care of yourself, Mr. Wallace," she said, patting his arm. "And if you have any problems, you be sure and give Dr. Frank a call. Any dizziness, headache, double vision—anything like that—you pick up a phone, you hear?"

Since he wasn't experiencing any of the above, it seemed safe enough to agree. "Sure. I'll do that."

LuWanda gave him a long, rather stern look. "Your health isn't something to take for granted, young man.

The doctor can't help you if he doesn't know what's wrong.''

It was entirely possible that he hadn't been doing as good a job at fooling everyone as he'd believed. She didn't know what his problem was, of course, but she obviously suspected there was something he was holding back. He wanted to get out of here before he somehow gave himself away. If he decided to reveal his memory loss to Dr. Frank, he wanted it to be *his* choice, and on his own terms.

On an impulse, he leaned over to brush a kiss against the nurse's soft, plump cheek, ignoring the protest from his cracked ribs. "Thank you for everything," he murmured.

He had the satisfaction of seeing the gruff-spoken, kindhearted tyrant blush as she hurried out of the room.

Sam turned to Serena, finding her watching him with a wary frown. "What?"

She shook her head and gathered plastic bags into her arms. "I'm going to be keeping a close eye on you, Sam Wallace."

She was reminding him that she still didn't quite trust him. Her words should have made him nervous— but instead he found the thought of being watched closely by Serena Schaffer rather intriguing....

Sam's first glimpse of the Schaffer house made him think again of that magical fictional town that was just a bit too flawless to be real. The tidy white frame house had neat black shutters and a front porch complete with big wooden rockers. Flowers bloomed in the yard. Even the weather contributed to the overall image of unreal perfection. Fluffy white clouds drifted lazily across a sky so blue it looked almost like a painted movie set.

This situation had the makings of a great horror film, he decided with wry whimsy. Two generous, seemingly kindhearted women living in a house straight out of a fairy tale, offering their hospitality to a man whose memory had been mysteriously wiped clean. A half dozen chilling scenarios played through his foggy mind from that beginning. Had he written horror stories in his previous life, or had he simply enjoyed reading them?

Serena followed the driveway around the side of the house and drove into a two-car garage at the back. A small import car was parked in the other bay, and Sam assumed it belonged to Marjorie. He climbed carefully out of Serena's low two-seater, his aching ribs and muscles protesting the movements. He was forced to steady himself with one hand against the vehicle as the garage swam dizzily around him for a moment.

Serena watched him over the hood of the car. "Are you all right?"

"I'm fine." He had answered more curtly than he intended, but he hated being so weak in front of her. If he ever found out who had done this to him... Even more important, he'd like to know *why*.

She insisted on carrying most of the packages—as if he were incapable of toting a few clothes in plastic bags, he thought in exasperation. Making an effort not to limp or cradle his throbbing sprained wrist, he followed Serena out of the garage and down a brick path. The guest house, as Marjorie had referred to it, was mostly hidden from the road, so this was Sam's first real look at it. Designed to match the style of the main house, it had a front porch just big enough to hold a wooden rocker.

Serena opened the front door with a key she then handed to Sam. Even as he accepted it, he was aware of the risk she was taking in giving it to him. He had no intention of taking advantage of her generosity—but she certainly had no way of knowing that.

The inside of the guest house was as tidy as the outside. Sam didn't have to be reminded that an elderly lady had lived here. The old-fashioned furniture, doilies and bric-a-brac would have given that away. Feeling like the bull in the china shop, he was pretty sure this was a far cry from the way he usually lived. Yet he was so relieved to be out of the hospital that he would happily coexist with a few doilies. "It's nice."

"Grandma called it 'cozy.' One bedroom, one bath, a kitchen and this living room. There's no phone, but you can come to our house if you need to make a call."

He shrugged. "There's no one I need to call."

"Mother stocked fresh linens and a few basic grocery items for you. If you need anything else, feel free to ask."

"I'm going to pay you and your mother back for everything," he said, turning to look at her. "The clothes, the food, the rent—you'll be reimbursed for all of it."

"We'll talk about that after you see about your medical bills." She piled the bags she had carried on one of the two wing chairs. And then she glanced his way, and her eyes narrowed. "Did Dr. Frank send any pain pills home with you?"

"A few, but I don't need one," he answered, trying

to ignore the throbbing in his head, his wrist, his rib cage—pretty much everywhere.

"I'll get you a glass of water. You find your pills."

Her tone didn't encourage argument, but he tried anyway. "I really don't—"

"Sam." She cut in firmly. "You won't recover unless you take care of yourself. If the pills will let you rest in relative comfort for the next few days, then you should take the pills."

He lifted an eyebrow. She sounded so determined, it seemed like a waste of breath to argue any further. "Okay. I'll take one."

His sudden capitulation apparently caught her off guard. "All right, then," she said after a moment, and turned toward the kitchen. "I'll be right back with the water."

Rather than waiting for her, he followed her into the kitchen, pulling the sample pack of pills out of his pocket. Like the living room, the kitchen was small and efficient, with not an inch of wasted space. Serena opened a cabinet and pulled out a plastic tumbler, which she filled with tap water. She jumped when she turned to find Sam only a step or two away. Water splashed over the side of the tumbler. "I didn't hear you behind me," she said unnecessarily.

"Sorry. I didn't mean to startle you."

"Did you find your pills?"

He opened his hand to show her the small yellow tablet in his palm.

Serena handed him the tumbler. He swallowed the pill, washed it down with half the water, then reached around her to set the glass on the counter. His arm brushed hers with the movement, and he felt her stiffen. Had the kitchen been bigger, he suspected she would have done a quick sidestep away from him. But since that move would have flattened her against the refrigerator, she stayed where she was. Sam was the one who moved away. As nice as it was to be close to her, he didn't want to give her a reason to regret offering him a place to recuperate.

"I'll leave you to settle in," she said, avoiding his eyes as she moved toward the doorway. "Mother's cooking a big lunch. She wanted me to invite you to join us—or, if you don't feel up to that, she'll bring a plate out to you. The meal should be ready by one, which will give you a couple of hours to rest first."

"Your mother doesn't have to cook for me. You said she stocked basic supplies. I'm perfectly capable of preparing a meal." At least, he assumed he was. He didn't actually remember cooking, but how hard could it be?

Serena's smile was suddenly ironic. "She lives for this sort of thing. And we are going to have lunch, anyway. It isn't that much trouble to make enough for one more."

"Then I would be pleased to join you. Thank you."

She was still moving toward the exit, putting as much distance between them as possible in the small space available. "We'll see you at one, then."

She was gone before he could respond. He supposed he couldn't blame her for being nervous around him, considering the circumstances. What he didn't understand was why, if she still had so many reservations about him, was she being so nice to him?

Marjorie fussed over her preparations for the meal until Serena finally couldn't stop herself from protesting. "Honestly, Mother, we aren't having a visiting foreign dignitary for lunch. It's only Sam Wallace—and we don't really know who he is."

"He's our guest," her mother replied as if that settled everything. "I hope he likes pot roast."

"Everyone likes your pot roast."

Marjorie slapped a hand to her cheek. "What if he's a vegetarian? I didn't think to ask."

"He isn't a vegetarian."

"How do you know?"

"Because I heard him wishing aloud for a steak when he was in the hospital. Vegetarians don't fantasize about steak."

"All I made for dessert is chocolate cake. Maybe I should throw together a quick fruit cobbler, in case he doesn't care for chocolate."

"Every normal person likes chocolate."

"Your sister doesn't."

"Yes, well, the operative word there is 'normal.' No normal woman of Kara's age would drop everything she's worked for to run off to Nashville with a country singer wanna-be she hardly knows."

Marjorie sighed. "You really should stop belittling Kara's decision, Serena. After all, it's her life. She has a right to choose how she wants to live it."

"I just wish she hadn't left me to deal with the life she abandoned here. Marvin, the newspaper—her stupid dog." Curled lazily in one corner of the kitchen, Walter lifted his head and yawned, as if to prove himself unaffected by Serena's habitual less-than-flattering description.

"Now, honey—"

Serena held up her hand in an apologetic gesture. It wasn't her mother's fault that Kara had run off on her quixotic quest, although it was Marjorie who had persuaded Serena to try to keep the newspaper running. It was just that Serena had been feeling overwhelmed lately by all the responsibility she had shouldered. And her concern about the unsettling vagabond who would soon be joining them for lunch wasn't settling her mind.

She could still almost feel the brush of Sam Wallace's arm against hers, and she still reacted with a funny little shiver of awareness that made her extremely nervous. She had no intention of following her sister's example and falling for an attractive stranger. Look where that had gotten Kara—her whole life upended so she could trail after the guy in pursuit of his dreams. Sam Wallace had no aspirations of musical stardom, as far as Serena knew, but he must be in search of something. Or running away from something. Why else would he be living on the road, drifting from place to place doing the occasional odd job, with no one or nothing permanent in his life?

Just as that question crossed her mind, someone knocked on the back door. At the same time, the front doorbell chimed, announcing another caller. Serena and Marjorie hesitated, looking at each other in mutual curiosity, and then Serena turned toward the kitchen door. "You let Sam in. I'll answer the front door."

Although she hadn't been expecting him, Serena wasn't particularly surprised to find Chief Dan Meadows on her doorstep. His dark scowl gave her a clue as to the purpose of his unannounced call. "I take it you aren't popping in for lunch."

"Tell me the rumors I heard aren't true," he said, ignoring her quip.

"That depends on what you heard."

"Have you and Marjorie invited Sam Wallace to live in your guest house?"

"You might as well come in," she said, holding the door wider and bracing herself for a lecture.

"So it *is* true." Dan was shaking his head when he passed her on his way to the living room. He'd already launched into his speech by the time she closed the door behind him. "Serena, I can't believe you've brought this man into your home. You don't know anything about him, except that someone beat the crap out of him and threw him in your ditch."

"He didn't have a place to stay."

"So you brought him home." He ran a hand through his hair, almost audibly grinding his teeth. "A total stranger with no ID, no money and a story that barely holds water."

"You have reason to believe he's been lying to us?"

"No," Dan admitted. "But I have no proof he's telling the truth, either," he added. "I can't find any-one who saw the truck he described, nor can I find any information on Sam Wallace."

"That's good, isn't it? That he doesn't have a rec-ord, I mean."

"Not as far as I can find out," Dan said cautiously. "But since he's given me nothing more than a name to work with, that's not saying much."

"What would you like, Chief? Fingerprints? Blood, maybe?"

The lazy drawl from behind them made Serena and Dan turn. Sam and Marjorie stood in the opposite doorway, Marjorie looking distressed, Sam noncha-lant.

"We could start with blood," Dan agreed in a mutter, not looking at all disconcerted to have been over-heard.

Marjorie planted her hands on her hips. "I can't believe what I'm hearing, Dan Meadows. Since when is it a crime to be the victim of a robbery? You should be out trying to catch the robbers who beat up Sam, not browbeating Sam for no good reason."

Marjorie's remonstration accomplished what Sam's sarcasm had not. Dan looked suddenly abashed. "I'm only saying there are parts of this guy's story that just don't add up. And he's told us nothing about who he is or where he comes from. How do we know he can be trusted?"

Marjorie wasn't appeased. "You're saying he faked his injuries? That would certainly be news to Dr. Frank."

"Of course he didn't fake his injuries. It's obvious he's been beaten. But…"

"Exactly." Marjorie dropped her hands with an air of finality. "Now, are you staying for lunch?"

"Well, I…"

"Serena, set another place. Dan will be joining us. But *only* if he's polite to our other guest," Marjorie added, giving Dan a stern look.

Serena couldn't help but smile at Dan's expression. He hadn't come for lunch, but she wasn't surprised that Marjorie had railroaded him into it. There was something about her mother that could turn even the most macho of males into toe-scuffing schoolboys. She had no doubt that both Sam and Dan would be on their best behavior during dinner. Marjorie was likely to send them to separate corners if they weren't. And Serena suspected they would go.

Smiling at that image, she went to obey her mother's instructions and set another place at the table.

Chapter Five

As Serena had predicted, Dan behaved well enough during the meal, but he didn't let etiquette stop him from grilling Sam at every opportunity—cordially, of course. Marjorie wouldn't have tolerated otherwise. "You said you were passing through looking for work when you accepted a ride from the men who robbed you. Where were you working before?"

Keeping his eyes on his plate, Sam cut into his tender pot roast. "Here and there. Oklahoma, most recently."

"Yeah? Where in Oklahoma?"

"Tulsa. Would you pass the salt, please, Serena?"

Serena's fingers brushed Sam's when she handed him the salt shaker. His felt cold. She wondered if he was still in pain. If so, he covered it well.

Dan kept his gaze on the other man. "And before Tulsa? Where did you grow up?"

"I moved around a lot. There isn't any particular place I call home. Mrs. Schaffer, this meal is delicious. The best I've had in longer than I can remember."

Marjorie beamed in response to Sam's compliment. "Thank you. I'm glad you're enjoying it."

Dan wasn't so easily distracted. "So, Sam—what types of jobs have you held? You're—what—thirty-two? Thirty-three?"

"Thirty-one."

"You must have had some interesting experiences in all those years on the road. Maybe you'd like to share some of them with us?"

"Dan—" Marjorie's voice held a note of warning.

He gave her a blandly innocent smile. "Just making lunch conversation, ma'am."

"I wouldn't want to bore everyone by droning on about my life," Sam remarked, his expression every bit as insouciant as Dan's. "Yours sounds more interesting. I've heard you've had a rash of break-ins around town lately. Have you made any headway in solving them?"

Serena couldn't help but be amused by the expression that crossed Dan's face. Sam's verbal arrow had hit the police chief directly in his professional ego. He replied stiffly. "No. We haven't made much progress yet. All I can do for now is follow the few leads I have and keep a close eye on anyone around here who seems suspicious."

"Don't you start again, Dan," Marjorie warned.

He flashed her a crooked grin, but made no promises.

As if to make sure the conversation stayed pleasant, Marjorie took charge of it. They spent the remainder of the meal talking about local current events. Sam didn't have much to contribute on that subject, of course, but Marjorie made sure he wasn't left out. By the time they'd finished the main course, Serena imagined that Sam could probably pass a pop quiz on Edstown trivia.

She was aware that she hadn't said much during lunch, offering only enough comments to keep her mother appeased. She had been unable to stop herself from watching Sam during the meal, studying his expressions and wondering about him. She tried to be subtle about it, examining him through her eyelashes while ostensibly concentrating on her food, but she couldn't seem to look away from him completely.

This absorption with him was beginning to worry her. She'd tried to rationalize it by telling herself that anyone would be intrigued by a man like Sam—so anonymous and mysterious. She'd never met anyone quite like him before; it was only natural that she was curious. But that didn't seem to fully explain her fascination with him.

Maybe it was because she had always found puzzles challenging—and Sam was definitely a puzzle. Everything she observed about him seemed to be at odds with what he'd told them. Young, handsome, obviously well educated, Sam Wallace, with his neatly manicured hands and lost, intelligent eyes, hardly fit her preconceptions of a rootless drifter.

She couldn't really blame Dan for his suspicions. It was obvious that there was a great deal Sam hadn't told them. She would like to know more about him. And while she told herself she merely wanted reassurance that he was trustworthy, she knew there was much more to her curiosity than that.

He looked up from his plate, and their gazes met

across the table. She had the sudden uncomfortable feeling that he could read her thoughts on her face. His thoughts were still a complete mystery to her.

"Is everyone ready for dessert?" Marjorie's question broke the moment, drawing Sam's attention away. Serena sank back in her seat, oddly disconcerted.

There was definitely something unsettling about this man Sam Wallace.

Sam was fully aware that Serena watched him all through lunch. She was trying to be subtle about it, but it was obvious to him, anyway. Dan Meadows kept him under close scrutiny, as well. Marjorie was the only one not watching him as if in concern that he might pocket the silverware if no one was looking.

He couldn't say it was a comfortable experience. But it was definitely interesting. And the food was either the best he'd ever eaten or just tasted that way in comparison to the hospital fare. After all, he couldn't remember any meals prior to waking up in the hospital.

He'd found himself wondering as the meal began whether there was something going on between Serena and the police chief. They certainly seemed to know each other well, interacting with the ease of familiarity. It didn't take him long to decide that they were friends, not lovers. He sensed affection between them, but little chemistry.

Some people might have found it rather amusing that a guy with a serious mental problem was analyzing other people's psyches, he thought with a wry, private smile. He doubted that either Serena or Dan would share the humor if they knew the truth.

His grim amusement faded quickly when Marjorie

entered the dining room with a big chocolate cake festooned with small burning candles. "Serena told me that today is your birthday," she said as she set the cake in front of Sam. "I hope you like chocolate cake."

Embarrassed, Sam cleared his throat. "Uh, yeah, I love chocolate cake. But you really didn't have to go to this much trouble."

She laughed, apparently amused that she'd rattled him. "Nonsense. Everyone deserves a birthday cake. Now make a wish and blow out the candles."

Acutely aware of Dan's too-observant eyes on him, Sam drew as deep a breath as his cracked ribs would allow and blew out the candles quickly.

"Oh, we were supposed to sing 'Happy Birthday' before you blew out the candles," Marjorie fussed.

Sam shook his head with a bit more force than necessary, making it start to ache again. "That isn't necessary. Really."

Serena took pity on him. "C'mon, Mother, are you trying to embarrass him right back into the hospital? Let's just serve the cake."

Dan very conspicuously remained silent, accepting his cake without commenting on the occasion it was intended to celebrate.

Though he didn't want to be impolite, Sam excused himself after dessert, explaining quite honestly that he had a headache. Marjorie wanted to hover a bit, but he was able to convince her that a couple more pain pills and a few hours rest would work wonders.

"Chief," he said to Meadows on his way out, "it's been a pleasure."

Dan looked ready to growl, but a quick glance at

Marjorie had him responding somewhat more civilly. "Yeah, well...take care of that head. And if there's anything I can do for you, Serena and Marjorie know how to get in touch with me. At all times," he added pointedly. "One call from them, and I'm here. Immediately."

Sam almost chuckled at the unveiled warning, but his head hurt so badly. Instead, he merely nodded, thanked Marjorie again for the meal and made his departure. He was certain Dan would start spouting dire warnings about him again, but he didn't feel like hanging around to defend himself. The only way he could prove his trustworthiness was by living quietly in the guest house, pulling his weight at the diner and making no waves in town.

As he entered the guest house, he found himself wondering how long he could go on living that way. Days? Weeks? Months? How long could he keep pretending that nothing was wrong, that this was normal routine for him?

Three weeks, he decided as he wandered into the bedroom. That seemed plenty long enough to recover from whatever head injury was causing his memory loss. If it hadn't come back at the end of those three weeks, he was definitely going to do something about it. He refused to take advantage of these unbelievably kind people for any longer than that.

But for now, he thought as he eased his aching body onto the bed, all he needed was a little rest. And maybe another pain pill.

As usual, the small parking lot of the Rainbow Café was full at noon on Monday. Serena circled twice before a vehicle pulled out, freeing a space. She was five minutes late for her luncheon appointment with Marvin Frieze, the managing editor of the newspaper. She would have chosen another venue for this conversation, but Marvin hadn't given her much choice, simply leaving a message with her secretary that he would be at the Rainbow Café if she wanted to join him.

As she'd predicted from the crowded parking lot, the café was bustling with the loyal lunch crowd, nearly every table filled. Serena recognized most of the patrons, but she didn't spot Marvin's snowy white head. Hoping he hadn't stood her up yet again, she spoke to the lanky, gum-chewing, sixty-something hostess. "I'm supposed to meet Marvin here. Have you seen him, Justine?"

"No. Did you check over at Gaylord's?"

Serena grimaced in response to the ironic reference to Marvin's worsening drinking habits. It seemed everyone in town was talking about it. "Just show him to my table when he arrives, will you?"

Justine snapped her gum, then grinned. "Sure thing."

Exchanging greetings with acquaintances along the way, Serena claimed one of the few empty tables, setting her purse beside her chair. She spotted her mother busily working the cash register at the exit door. They waved, but Marjorie was too busy to stop and visit just then. Ever since two of her employees had left on short notice, things had been hectic in the diner. It was no wonder Marjorie was getting desperate enough to offer jobs to just about anyone.

Almost as if that thought had conjured him up, Sam Wallace appeared at her table, looking more like a battered prizefighter than a waiter. His unarguably handsome face was still bruised and slightly swollen.

The small white bandage at his right temple hid the stitches there, and his injured left wrist was supported by a Velcro-fastened brace. He gave her a smile. "What would you like to drink, Ms. Schaffer?"

It took her a moment to respond. His sudden appearance had caught her off guard. She really hadn't expected to see him here barely twenty-four hours after his release from the hospital. She hadn't seen any sign of activity from the guest house when she'd left for her office earlier that morning. He must have ridden to the café with Marjorie an hour or so after Serena's departure. She would bet that he was in considerable discomfort with this physical activity, if not outright pain.

Maybe he really was sincere about working to pay back the debts he incurred. Certainly no one would have blamed him for taking a few days off to recuperate. The guy still looked like he'd fall over in a strong wind, for Pete's sake. "What are you doing here?"

He lifted his eyebrows, shifting the bandage at his temple. "I work here."

"I meant, why are you here today? Surely Dr. Frank hasn't cleared you to go to work so soon."

Sam shrugged. "I didn't ask him. I know what I'm capable of doing—and your mother obviously accepts that, since she put me straight to work when I asked to get started."

Marjorie was desperate enough to put a trained monkey to work, Serena thought, glancing wryly around the almost frantically busy diner. It was all Justine and Shameka, the other server, could do to keep up. "Just be careful not to overdo it. You had a head injury. Not to mention all the—"

"Thanks for the concern, but I'll be fine. Now, can I get you something to drink? Or are you ready to order your food? Some of the other customers are looking restless."

She noticed that his hands were empty. "Don't you need an order pad?"

"No." His expression was suddenly ironic—as if he were enjoying a private joke. "It turns out I have a very good memory for keeping track of orders."

"Oh. Well, that's...good, I guess."

"Hey, Sam. Could I have some more coffee here?" someone called from a table nearby.

"Serena?" he prodded, after waving an acknowledgement toward the other table.

"I'll just have a glass of ice water now. I'm expecting someone to join me. I'll order when he arrives."

He nodded and moved away. After refilling coffees at several tables, he returned to set a glass of water in front of Serena. "The boyfriend seems to be running late," he remarked, nodding toward the empty chair across from her.

"The *employee* who is joining me is sixty-five years old and chronically late," she replied, and then wondered why she'd bothered to correct him.

Sam's rather smug smile let her know that he had been fishing for information, probably out of nothing more than idle curiosity. She had to admit he was pretty good at it. "Give me a sign when you're ready to order," he said, and then moved on to another table.

While she waited for Marvin, she watched Sam at work. Of *course* she watched him, she thought wryly—that seemed to be all she did when he was around. But it was interesting. He didn't seem to have a lot of experience at waiting tables, but what he lacked in skill, he made up for in hustle. Despite his injuries, he never seemed to slow down. Despite being a newcomer to the area, he chatted comfortably with the customers. They eyed his bruises, of course, but seemed to accept his presence easily enough; nearly everyone had heard about the hapless drifter who'd been robbed and dumped in Serena's ditch. And since everyone knew of Marjorie's penchant for helping those in need, no one seemed particularly surprised to see Sam working at her diner.

Edstown had a history of opening its arms to eccentrics and oddballs, Serena mused. Sam Wallace seemed to fit in to both those categories.

She'd been waiting at the table for twenty minutes and had emptied two glasses of ice water before she conceded that Marvin was a no-show. Again. "Looks like your employee had something come up," Sam commented, filling her glass again.

"My soon-to-be-*ex*-employee," Serena muttered, finally accepting the inevitable. She had to let Marvin go—if she could ever catch up with him long enough to tell him.

"What's your soon-to-be-ex-employee's job?"

"Managing editor of the *Evening Star,* the town newspaper. My family has owned the paper for several generations, but I've only been lucky enough to run it for the past six months. Now it looks like I'm going to have to hire a new editor."

"Sorry to hear that. Want some lunch now?"

She nodded. "As a matter of fact, I'm starving. I'll have a turkey sandwich and a fruit salad."

"Excellent choice, madam. I'll bring that right out to you."

Taking advantage of a respite as the lunch crowd thinned, Marjorie left Justine at the register and crossed the room to Serena's table, sinking into the empty chair. "Justine said you were expecting Marvin to join you for lunch."

"He stood me up."

Frowning in concern, Marjorie suggested, "Perhaps things got hectic at the newspaper and he couldn't get away."

"Or perhaps he decided to have a liquid appetizer and forgot all about our appointment."

Sighing regretfully, Marjorie nodded. "I suppose that's possible."

"I'm going to have to let him go, Mom."

"Oh, Serena. Can't you give him another chance?"

"How many chances should I give him? A dozen? A hundred? Should I wait until he puts Great-granddad's paper completely out of business? Because I have to tell you, it's hanging on by a very thin thread now."

"It's that bad?"

Serena saw no reason to sugarcoat her answer. "It's that bad. Advertising revenues are down, and since Marvin has apparently lost all interest in his job, the paper seems to have no focus at all these days. Riley's tried to fill in, but he has his own duties to perform, and he's falling behind in all of them. You know he isn't crazy about schedules and responsibilities, anyway. He only works at the paper to make enough to support his writing habit."

"Do you think he's ever going to finish that novel he's been working on for so long?"

Serena shrugged. "Who knows? But it makes a great excuse for him to avoid extra duties. I approached him about taking over as managing editor—he's certainly qualified, even with his shortcomings—but he wants no part of it. He told me to hire someone else and he'll continue to do the job he's been doing, at least until he finishes and sells his great novel.''

''What about Lindsey? She's a trained journalist.''

''Yes, and she's a very good reporter. Too good for our paper, probably. She should be working in one of the bigger markets, moving up the editorial ladder there. But she isn't ready to take over the *Evening Star*. She's too young, too impulsive, too impatient with the politics of business management. As long as she's content to cover local news, that's what I would like for her to do. We've got a high school junior covering local sports and a retired home economics teacher writing the weekly food column. There's no one currently on staff, other than Riley, who's qualified as managing editor. I'll have to hire from outside.''

''Then that's what you'll do,'' Marjorie said firmly. ''As fond as I am of Marvin, we can't let him destroy our family heritage.''

Marjorie had always seen the little paper in that romantic light.

Sam slid Serena's lunch in front of her. ''Is there anything else I can get for you?''

She eyed the dark circles forming beneath his eyes. ''I think what you'd better do is go sit down for a while. You're trying to do too much today.''

''Serena's right, Sam. The busiest time is over. Justine and Shameka and I can handle it from here. You've done a wonderful job on your first day, but why don't you rest until I can drive you home?''

A man at the next table gestured to get Sam's attention. "How about some coconut pie over here?"

Sam nodded toward the other table, then flashed Serena and Marjorie a smile. "I'll rest later. Right now I have pie to serve."

Serena frowned at her mother. "You really shouldn't have encouraged him to work today. It's too soon. He has to be in pain."

"You'd never know it from watching him. He's not slowed down since we arrived this morning."

"Mother, only yesterday he was in the hospital with a concussion, broken ribs and a sprained wrist. It's absurd that he's working today. He should have taken off at least a few days to recuperate."

"I suggested that this morning. He said he's tired of lying around doing nothing and he wants to get his debts paid off as soon as possible."

"And if he collapses on the job? Have you considered that you could be liable under those circumstances?"

"In the first place, I'm not going to collapse. In the second, I wouldn't blame your mother if I did."

Serena hadn't heard Sam behind her until he spoke. She turned her frown at him, hiding her slight embarrassment at being overheard. "I still think you're trying to do too much too soon."

"And I thank you for your concern," he replied, his firm tone making it clear that he wasn't in the market for advice.

With that, he moved on to another table. Serena sighed and pushed away her mostly empty plate. "Okay, I give up."

"Don't worry about Sam, dear. I'll make sure he doesn't overdo it."

Serena gave what she hoped would pass for a negligent shrug. "Why should I worry about him? I have my own problems to deal with. And I have a meeting with a client in twenty minutes, so I'd better be on my way."

"Are you going to talk to Marvin today?"

Serena winced. "That depends on whether I can find him—and if he's sober enough to understand me when I do."

"I know this won't be easy for you, dear. But if it must be done to save the paper, then you have no other choice."

"I know."

"Just try to be kind about it, will you? Don't be an attorney—be a sympathetic friend."

Serena barely resisted rolling her eyes. "I'm not sure Marvin is going to think of me as any kind of friend while I'm threatening to fire him, Mother. But I'll try."

She was still mulling over her mother's advice when she drove out of the diner's parking lot a few minutes later. She had tried to be a sympathetic friend to Marvin, and it hadn't worked. No amount of advice or lenience or understanding had accomplished anything with him. Now she was going to have to be something he had never allowed her to be—his boss. As much as she dreaded it, she was prepared to do what she had to do.

She might never forgive Kara for putting her in this painful situation, she thought, practically seething with pent-up anger and disappointment in her older sister.

Chapter Six

Often when she had trouble sleeping, Serena wandered outside, where she let the sounds and scents of nighttime soothe her. Though she doubted it would help on this particular night, she stepped out the door at just after midnight wearing a T-shirt, shorts and sandals and carrying a cup of herbal tea. She headed for the yard swing beside her mother's rose garden, her favorite place to sit on balmy nights.

Tonight someone else was already sitting in her swing.

"Looks like you've found me again, Ms. Schaffer," Sam drawled, looking at her from the shadows of the covered swing.

Her pulse jumped, as it always seemed to do when she encountered this man. She kept trying to attribute it to natural wariness of a mysterious stranger, but she was aware there was more to it than that. She would be lying to herself if she denied the attraction that she felt for him—and she tried to always be brutally honest with herself. It seemed much more sensible in the long run than self-deception.

She tried to speak with the same nonchalant tone he'd used. "At least you're conscious this time. What are you doing?"

"I couldn't sleep. Came out for some fresh air. You?"

"Same thing," she admitted.

He scooted to one side of the swing and patted the seat next to him. "There's room for two." When she hesitated, he murmured, "Scared?"

To prove how ridiculous that was, she sank onto the swing beside him, carefully balancing her cup of tea. Sam steadied the swing, letting it sway gently again only when he was sure she was settled. "It's nice out here. The roses smell good."

"My mother takes care of the roses. They're sort of her hobby." The rich scents from the blooms surrounded the swing like a fragrant cloud—not overpowering, just pleasant. Stars sparkled brilliantly in the blue-black sky, and a half moon floated serenely among them. As the old saying went, it was a night made for romance—or in this case, Serena corrected herself quickly, a midnight chat with a stranger.

"What about you, Serena? Do you have any hobbies?"

"I haven't really had time for hobbies lately, though I like to read when I have a few spare minutes. And you?"

He shrugged. "I've done a little mountain climbing. Race car driving. Sky diving. Gold mining. Rodeo."

She'd bet the cup of tea in her hand that he was

making those answers up as he went along. He must really enjoy putting her on, since he did it so often. "Rodeo?" she repeated, blandly playing along. "I *thought* I detected a hint of Texas in your accent."

He seemed to find that comment intriguing. "You think I have a Texas accent?"

"Yes, at least a slight one. Have you spent a lot of time there?"

"Uh—yeah. Sure. That's where I spent the last few years."

"I thought you said you came here from Oklahoma."

"I said I was most recently in Tulsa," he corrected her after a momentary pause. "I wasn't there very long."

He seemed determined to be as vague as possible about his background—which, of course, only renewed her uneasiness about him. "You got restless there?"

"I suppose so."

She sipped her tea, then glanced sideways at him again. "How are you feeling?"

"Okay. Why?"

"I thought you would surely collapse from working a full shift at the diner so soon after leaving the hospital. But here you are, still wide awake and doing fine."

"Honestly?" His tone was suddenly rueful. "I *did* collapse—the minute I walked into the guest house after work. Fell facedown in bed and zonked out. I didn't stir until your mom brought dinner out to me— which she didn't have to do, by the way. I'm not as tired now, but every inch of my body aches."

Serena nodded in satisfaction—not because he was

in pain, but because she'd been right about him trying to do too much too soon. "I assume you'll be taking tomorrow off to rest?"

"Your assumption is incorrect. I made it through today, and it will be easier tomorrow."

"Why do you need to push yourself so hard?"

"Because I need the money," he answered simply. "I've only been in this town a few days and it seems like I owe everyone here. Before I move on, I'd like to rectify that."

The man was obsessed with paying off his debts. Admirable, she conceded, but it shouldn't be at the expense of his health. Knowing she would be wasting her breath to argue with him yet again, she let it go.

"So what's keeping *you* awake tonight?" As Sam spoke, he shifted slightly on the swing, causing his leg to brush lightly against hers. He moved it immediately away, but the sensation remained—and Serena suspected the memory of that contact could keep her awake for the rest of the night, if she allowed herself to dwell on her wholly unexpected, almost electrified reaction.

She made an effort to answer him coherently. "I had to have a talk with a longtime employee this afternoon. It was a...difficult scene."

"Let me guess. You were tough and hard-nosed because you had to be, but now you're tearing yourself up about it because you're really softer inside than you pretend to be most of the time."

"What makes you say that?"

"Maybe I'm getting to know you better than you think."

"Or maybe you just think you are."

He chuckled. "Maybe. So, was I right?"

"You were right," she said with a sigh of resignation. "I've been feeling guilty all evening, even though I had no other choice. And I know I should have fired him, rather than just threatened to do so. I've been worrying about the future of the paper because the managing editor isn't holding up his responsibilities. I've convinced the assistant editor to fill in the slack, but he made me promise I'd either get Marvin back to work or find someone else to replace him. Soon."

"He doesn't want the job himself?"

"No. He's been writing the great American novel for about ten years now and he said he needs plenty of free time to finish it. The managing editor position is too time-consuming and responsibility-intensive for Riley to want it."

"Lazy?"

"Oh, no, he's not lazy. Just…difficult to pin down. Riley's a free spirit. You should identify with that," she added. It occurred to her that Riley would probably live a drifter's existence himself if it weren't for the novel that had been his anchor for so long.

"Why don't *you* handle the job? What, exactly, do you do at the newspaper?"

She lifted an eyebrow. "Very little. My law practice keeps me too busy to—"

The swing jerked. "Your *what?*"

Surprised, she blinked at him. "Surely you know I'm an attorney."

"No, I didn't know that. I guess it never came up."

She could tell from his tone that he wasn't pleased with the information. "What have you got against attorneys?"

He paused a moment before he answered. "I'm not sure."

"Oh, *that* makes sense." Had she ever met a more perplexing male?

"Sorry, there's just something about lawyers..."

"I've heard all the jokes, so don't waste your breath. I know why sharks won't eat lawyers—professional courtesy. I know what you call a hundred lawyers at the bottom of the ocean—a good start. I know why the lawyer crossed the road—to chase the ambulance on the other side. Have I missed any?"

His scowl had changed to a reluctant smile. "Maybe a few."

"Yes, well, who would you call to protect your rights in a lawsuit? A plumber? Who would you turn to if you were mistakenly arrested for a crime? A bank teller?"

"Okay, I'll admit that lawyers have their uses. I was just surprised, that's all. I thought the newspaper was your only job."

"No. Actually, I didn't even want that job. My father, who was also an attorney, supervised the operation of the newspaper until his unexpected death a year ago. My sister, Kara, had always planned to take over the paper, but she recently had a change of heart. Since my mother didn't feel qualified, especially with the demands of her diner, that left me. I tried to talk Mother into letting me sell, but the paper's been in our family so long she wouldn't hear of it."

"So you're doing all this to please your mother?"

"I guess I am," she answered with a faint sigh. "My mother seems to think we'd be letting down my father if we sold the paper. Unlike my sister, I can't do that to her now."

"Whoa. I heard some hostility toward your sister there."

"She dropped all her responsibilities and ran off on some harebrained mission to find musical stardom for her boyfriend. She didn't think about anyone but herself. You bet I'm feeling hostile toward her, especially tonight, after dealing with yet another unpleasant chore that should have been hers."

"You're angry with her for pursuing a dream?"

Worded like that, it sounded petty and selfish. "If it were *her* dream, I'd be more sympathetic. But it's some guy's dream she's chasing, not her own. And she didn't give a thought to those of us left behind to clean up after her."

"She loves the guy?"

"She says she does."

Sam shrugged. "Then maybe her dream is to accomplish something with someone she loves."

"If that's true, I hope her dream isn't shattered when he dumps her for someone more likely to get him what he wants."

"You think he's a user?"

Serena started to answer, then hesitated. "I don't know," she confessed after a moment. "He and Kara had a whirlwind courtship before they took off for Nashville, and I didn't have a chance to get to know him very well. He seemed very fond of Kara, but—"

"But cynical Serena, the small-town lawyer, can't help questioning his motives and worrying about his character," Sam cut in. "Much the way the good police chief feels about *me*."

"I fail to see any similarities."

Sam laughed softly and tugged at a strand of her

hair. "Do you ever really fool anyone with that prim and prissy tone?"

Suddenly disconcerted, she looked away from him, noting that her cup was empty. She didn't even remember finishing the tea. "If we're going to work tomorrow, we should probably try to get some sleep first."

"You're right, of course." He stood, rocking the swing, then turned to hold out a hand to her.

To prove again that he didn't intimidate her, Serena placed her hand in his and allowed him to assist her out of the swing. He didn't immediately release her, but stood smiling at her in the moonlight.

"What?" she asked, frowning at him.

"Nothing. I've just enjoyed talking with you."

She wasn't quite sure how to respond to that, especially since her pulse was suddenly thrumming and her heart seemed to have added an extra beat. She warned herself not to be influenced by the intimate atmosphere of the night and the roses. Not to mention the handsome, intriguingly enigmatic man holding her hand. "I really should go in."

He seemed to be staring at her mouth, though it was hard to tell since he was silhouetted against the golden moon. His blond hair glinted in the moonlight, and she was forced to moisten her lips, which had gone dry for some reason.

Sam made a faint sound—she wasn't sure if he groaned or cleared his throat—and then he released her hand and stepped back. "Yes," he muttered, his voice gruff, "you should definitely go in now."

She found herself lingering for another moment. "Do you have any more pain pills to take if you need one?"

"I've replaced the prescription pills with over-the-counter pain relievers. I'm okay."

He would say that no matter how he felt, she suspected. Sam was certainly not a complainer. "Well... good night."

"Good night, Serena. Sleep well."

She turned and walked toward the house, keeping her steps measured and unhurried. She didn't want to look as though she was running away from him—even though that was exactly the way she felt.

She couldn't help wondering what it would have been like to have been kissed by Sam Wallace in the moon-washed rose garden. And then she scolded herself for sounding all too much like her sister, who had allowed a romantic infatuation to turn her life—and her family's lives—completely upside down. That was one example Serena had no intention of following.

Sam's second day at work was no less demanding than the first, but he found it somewhat less difficult to get through his shift. The day after was even easier, as was the day after that. Either his injuries were healing or he was learning to deal with them better, but he wasn't as exhausted when Marjorie drove him home on Friday. Telling him she had a garden club meeting to attend that afternoon, she asked him if he would be all right on his own, and he had to gently remind her that he was perfectly capable of taking care of himself.

He appreciated Marjorie's kindness to him, but he was beginning to feel a bit smothered by her solicitousness. Without a vehicle or money, he was completely dependent on Marjorie's generosity. He wasn't sure, of course, but he sensed this wasn't a normal condition for him. If he felt this proud and self-sufficient now, it stood to reason he'd have been the same prior to his accident, didn't it?

He rested for a while, then took a hot shower. Dressed in clean clothes, he wandered into the kitchen and put a cup of water in the microwave to heat for instant coffee. While the water heated, he studied his reflection in the small, decorative mirror mounted on the wall beside the back door. The scrapes and bruises were fading, giving him a better idea of what he usually looked like. Blond hair, blue eyes, regular features—nothing out of the ordinary, in his opinion. Nothing to give him a clue as to who he was or where he came from.

Because he was finding it increasingly uncomfortable to try to retrieve memories that were beginning to seem permanently lost to him, he turned his thoughts to Serena as he carried his coffee to the table. Through the kitchen window, he could see the rose garden and the swing where he and Serena had shared such a pleasant midnight interlude Monday evening. Well, pleasant except for one jarring discovery.

He still wasn't quite sure why it had bothered him so badly to find out that Serena was a lawyer. Even now, his reaction to the word was immediate and negative. He didn't understand why—it was obviously connected to those lost memories. Trying to solve the puzzle only made his head ache, so he concentrated instead on remembering the way Serena's hand had felt in his when he'd helped her out of the swing. The way her pretty oval face had looked in the moonlight, her eyes glistening, her lips moist and parted. He'd wanted to kiss her so badly he'd ached—and that pain had had nothing to do with his injuries.

He wondered what her reaction would have been had she known what he was thinking. Or *had* she somehow known? Was that why she'd been avoiding him ever since?

She thought of him as a stranger—which, of course, he was. Even to himself. What could an attractive young attorney from a respectable small town see in a battered, penniless drifter—if that's what he was? And even if she was interested, he was hardly in a position to pursue anything more than a casual friendship. For all he knew, he had a wife and a houseful of kids somewhere—though he found that very difficult to believe. He just didn't feel married, somehow.

Even *he* was aware how lame that sounded, he thought with a disgusted shake of his head.

Since thinking of Serena was becoming as uncomfortable as trying to remember his past, he pushed the thoughts aside and carried his empty cup to the sink. The remaining hours of the day stretched ahead of him, empty and uninteresting. Restlessness tugged at him, drawing him toward the door. Maybe if he got out, walked around town for a while, he might accidentally stumble onto a clue about his past. Some trigger that would bring the memories flooding back—a sight, a sound, a smell, anything. If nothing else, at least he'd be getting outside.

It was only a mile or so from the house to downtown Edstown. Sam could easily walk to the diner, though Marjorie had insisted he ride with her. Keeping his pace leisurely, he spent the afternoon exploring, passing through the quiet residential section in which the Schaffer home was located, past a tidy trailer park and into the downtown area with its old stone buildings and dusty glass storefronts. He nodded to a few townspeople he'd seen in the diner. The sidewalks weren't exactly crowded, but they weren't empty, either.

Marjorie had explained that after years of deterioration, the downtown area had experienced a resurgence recently. Along with the banks and offices that had been there for decades, new businesses had opened in long-vacant buildings—a couple of antique stores, a coffee shop and bakery, a florist and a children's clothing store. Charming, in a vintage Americana way, but there was nothing remotely familiar about any of it to him.

Studying the fluttering blue-and-white awning over the children's store, he strained for any clue about where he might have come from. He glanced at the summer sky over the one- and two-story buildings and mentally filled it with towering skyscrapers. He was remembering a large city, obviously. But where? Was the flash of memory merely a place he'd visited, or was it home for him?

His head began to pound, as it always did when he tried to force the memories. It had become a matter of self-defense to mentally flinch away from the effort and concentrate only on the present. He did so, even though there were only two weeks remaining until his self-imposed deadline for admitting the truth.

An oddly shaped stone building at the end of the block housed an old-fashioned candy store called Sweets 'n' Treats. Sam had noticed it before, but had yet to see enough customers there to indicate that business was thriving. He knew that many small businesses closed within the first couple of years of operation—one of those useless trivia facts he'd retained

when his more vital memories had been wiped clean—
and this store looked as though it might be in trouble.

He almost turned around before he spotted the
young boy pressed against the glass at the very end of
the store. The kid was scrawny, probably no more than
ten or eleven and dressed in faded hand-me-down
clothes. Sandy hair in need of a trim tumbled over his
forehead and ears, and his sneakers looked ready for
the trash bin. Sam could almost see the boy's mouth
watering as he gazed at the colorfully displayed can-
dies inside the store. Without thinking, he said,
"Looks good, doesn't it?"

Obviously startled, the boy whipped his head
around. The ugly bruise that covered the left side of
his face made Sam frown even as he remembered that
he really shouldn't talk to kids he didn't know. As
innocuous as the overture had been, he didn't need
Chief Meadows pegging him as a potential pervert in
addition to whatever else he already suspected.

After a moment during which the boy seemed to
debate the wisdom of talking to a stranger, he finally
nodded and said, "It *all* looks good."

Sam glanced at the window display. "I used to like
those long red licorice whips when I was a kid." The
statement felt oddly right. So much so that it was probably true.

"I like those, too," the boy agreed. "But my fa-
vorites are those big coiled lollipops. They last *for-
ever*."

Eying the lollipop that was nearly as big as the
boy's head, Sam chuckled. "It would definitely take
a while to finish one of those."

He was tempted to offer to buy the boy one of the
treats—Marjorie had insisted on giving him a small

advance against his salary so he'd have some cash—but he couldn't figure out how to make the offer without destroying every lesson the kid should have been taught about accepting gifts from strangers. He hated the necessity of teaching those lessons, but he knew they were justified.

The boy sighed and stepped away from the window. "I gotta go. My, uh, stepdad is waiting for me at the muffler shop."

The muffler shop was one street over. Sam had spotted it during his walk. That explained what the kid was doing alone on the streets of downtown. "Nice talking to you."

"Yeah. See ya, mister." The kid started to walk away, then turned again. "What's your name?"

"I've been answering to Sam."

Nodding gravely, the boy seemed to find nothing particularly odd about Sam's choice of words. "My name's Zach."

"Nice to meet you."

"Bye, Sam."

"Bye, Zach."

Sam watched as Zach rushed off. Something about the kid had tugged at Sam's memory. What made him suspect the boy was unhappy, that he wasn't returning to a loving, supportive home? What caused him to worry that the bruise on that freckled face hadn't been caused by a boyhood tumble but by an angry hand? Why could he almost feel that careless swipe of hand against his own face?

"Hey, Sam. What's up?"

The lazy drawl made him turn. With a sense of inevitability, he said, "Chief Meadows."

"You're looking better than the last time I saw you."

"Thanks—I think."

"Doing some sightseeing?"

"A bit. Nice town you've got here."

Dan seemed to take the comment as a personal compliment. "Thanks."

"Did you happen to notice the boy I was just talking to?"

"I noticed."

Of course he had. Sam doubted that very much in this town escaped the police chief's attention. "He said his name is Zach. Do you know him?"

"I recognized him, I don't know every kid in town, of course, but I've seen that one a couple of times."

"Professionally?"

"Why do you ask?"

"His face was bruised. Maybe he just fell off his bike, but it looked a little suspicious."

Dan frowned and looked in the direction in which the boy had disappeared. "I'll try to find an excuse to check on him later."

"So there *is* a problem?" Sam thought of the general air of dejectedness he'd detected in the boy's posture.

"Let's just say that not every adult in Edstown is a model citizen."

"He seemed like a nice kid."

"I'll check up on him," Dan promised again, and Sam got the message that he needn't pursue the matter any further. "How are things going at the diner?"

"Busy. Marjorie's got a thriving business there."

"Yeah. The Rainbow Café's the place to go for lunch. Good breakfast crowd, too."

"Tell me about it. I can't keep the coffee cups filled fast enough."

Dan scratched his chin. "I've got to admit, I never would have pegged you as a busboy."

Refusing to take offense, Sam only shrugged. "I'm also a waiter. And a dishwasher when necessary."

"You're content with that?"

"For now. At least until I'm out of debt and back to full speed." Which included the return of his memory, of course, he added silently.

"Just so you know, I haven't given up on catching the guys who mugged you. I'm still pursuing every lead, no matter how slim, but it looks like your attackers have left the area."

Flooded with guilt as he thought of the time Dan had wasted chasing this particular wild goose, Sam cleared his throat. When he'd impulsively concocted that tale, he'd been too groggy from medication and trauma, and dazed by the realization that his memory was gone, to give much thought to repercussions. It had been incredibly stupid on his part, as so many of his actions had been since Serena found him.

"About those guys, Chief," he began, only to be interrupted by a woman's husky voice.

"Dan! Here you are. I've been looking all over for you."

For the first time, Sam saw the police chief look flustered—but only for a moment. Whatever the expression had meant, Dan masked it immediately. "Hey, Lindsey. What's the big emergency this time?"

The petite redhead studied both men with curious bright green eyes, then focused on Sam. "You must be Serena's stranger."

He had to smile at her wording. "I'm Sam Wallace."

"Lindsey Gray." She held out her hand. "I've been wanting to talk to you, but Serena wouldn't let me."

"Probably afraid you'd worry him back into the hospital with your nosy questions," Dan muttered.

Lindsey shot him a look, but spoke again to Sam. "I'm a reporter for the *Evening Star*. I'd like to talk to you about what happened—the mugging, I mean. The story I ran about you was awfully sketchy, and I'd like more details. We don't see that sort of crime around here very often and I—"

"I'd rather not."

She blinked in response to Sam's firm interjection. "I understand there are some questions you'd probably rather not answer, but—"

"I'd rather not be interviewed. Period."

"But—"

"I really have nothing more to tell you," he explained. "I remember very few details about the attack, and everything else is part of an ongoing police investigation. That leaves only my personal life to talk about, and I doubt you'd find that interesting enough for an article."

"Oh, but I—"

"It was very nice meeting you, Ms. Gray. Come into the Rainbow Café sometime and I'll buy you a cup of coffee. Chief, it was a pleasure to see you, as always. Oh, and don't forget to check on that matter I mentioned to you, will you?"

"Are you sure I can't give you a lift home?" Dan looked eager to have an excuse to escape the determined reporter.

Lindsey protested, "But, Dan, I want to talk to you."

Rather enjoying the cocky police chief's predicament, Sam grinned. "Thanks for the offer, but I'm enjoying the exercise. And besides, I wouldn't want to take you away from Ms. Gray's questions."

Dan gave him a rather comical look that promised he would get even for this somehow.

"If you change your mind about talking to me," Lindsey began to say to Sam.

"I won't," he assured her. "Not for an interview, anyway. But I meant what I said about that cup of coffee."

He heard her sigh gustily behind him when he turned to walk away. And then she complained to Dan, "That man never let me finish a sentence."

"I wish he'd teach *me* that trick," Sam heard Dan grumble. "What is it you want now, Lindsey?"

Sam didn't linger long enough to hear her reply. He had decided to stop by the library, maybe do a little research on amnesia. It was long past time he took an active part in finding out just what was wrong with him and what he should be doing about it—besides lying to everyone he met.

Chapter Seven

It was Walter who led Serena to Sam again Saturday afternoon. She'd let the dog out to take care of nature, and he'd headed straight for the fence at the back of the property. Before she could stop him, he'd wriggled underneath by way of a hole he'd discovered when Serena hadn't been watching. He was gone before she could yell his name.

"Son of a..." Finishing the curse beneath her breath, she drew a deep breath and let herself out the back gate, prepared for a chase. "I should let him get lost, see how he likes eating out of garbage cans and dodging pickup trucks. If I ever catch him, I swear I'm going to give him away. Why should I have to be responsible for a dog I never wanted? *Walter,* get your scrawny butt back in the yard before I—"

"You think his butt is scrawny?" Sam stepped out

of the trees beside the road, carrying the squirming dog in his arms. "He certainly feels chunky enough."

Her hand on her pounding heart, Serena glared at him. "Where did you come from?"

"I walked down to the lake. Walter, here, met me coming back."

"You walked all the way to the lake?"

"All the way? Serena, it's only a couple of miles."

He didn't even looked winded, she noted. His bruises had faded, and the assorted cuts and scrapes that had marred his face were almost healed. She'd thought him good-looking before—he was almost breathtakingly so now. Who *was* this golden-haired, blue-eyed Adonis wearing discount store clothes, holding a squirming mutt and giving her a smile that had her heart tripping all over itself? "I'm, uh, glad you've recovered so finely—er, so well."

"Lots of rest, fresh air and plenty of your mother's good cooking. Better than any treatment I received in the hospital."

Walter wiggled and tried to lick Sam's face. Sam chuckled. "We'd better get this guy back to the house. I'll see if I can repair the fence to keep him from making another dash for freedom."

She nodded and turned toward the row of fences that marked the back of her neighborhood. There were five houses on her street, all with large yards. The house in which she'd spent most of her life was at the end of the street. She could see the second story over the top of the wooden fence her father had built. The window on the right marked her bedroom, still filled with the mahogany furniture she'd picked out for her seventeenth birthday. Except for the years she'd spent away at college and law school and the apartment she'd maintained for a while afterward, she'd lived her whole life in that house.

How dull must that seem to a man who drifted from one place to another as the mood struck him, never staying anywhere long enough to put down roots?

Not that she envied Sam's lifestyle, she assured herself hastily. She still thought Kara was nuts to have left everything familiar to embark on a crazy quest with a man she hardly knew. Serena was perfectly content with her own life just the way it was. Except for Kara's dog, of course, she added with a dark look at the goofy mutt.

"Funny about this town," Sam mused as they went through the back gate into the big yard that was almost filled with the garage, the guest house and Marjorie's rose gardens. "Within a five-mile radius, you've got woods, neighborhoods ranging from tiny tract houses to upscale homes to trailer parks, a lake and a business section. It's like a microcosm of a society—like one of those toy play sets."

"Haven't you ever spent any time in small towns? They're all pretty much like that."

A funny expression crossed his face. "I guess I haven't."

"You guess? You don't know?"

Seeing that Serena had the gate secured, Sam set Walter on the ground. The dog bounced around their feet for a minute, then headed straight for the hole where he'd gotten through the fence before. Sam caught him, then pushed him into Serena's arms. "You'd better put him in the house while I fix the fence or he'll be out again."

"You don't have to do this, you know."

"I don't mind helping out." He shrugged. "It gives

me something useful to do. Actually, I've already offered to do some yard work and maintenance around the place, but your mother insisted I wait until I've been out of the hospital for a week before starting. That week is up tomorrow.''

Again, he surprised her with his determination to pull his own weight. Not even Dan could accuse him of taking advantage of anyone so far. Sam worked to repay every favor that had been done for him. Marjorie claimed he was one of the best employees she'd hired in a long time. Thinking of his uncallused, neatly manicured hands, she wondered again what kind of work he usually did to support himself. She still found it hard to believe he'd spent much time at manual labor.

By the time she returned after locking up the dog, Sam had fetched some tools and several extra boards that had been stacked in one corner of the garage. She noticed that he wielded the hammer rather awkwardly, reinforcing her suspicions about his lack of experience as a handyman, but he repaired the fence more quickly than she could have done it. The hammer slipped only once, landing squarely on his thumb and causing him to mutter a curse for which he immediately apologized.

''Is your thumb okay?'' she asked, stifling a smile.

''Yeah. If it's stupid enough to get under a hammer, it deserves to be flattened,'' he quipped with a crooked grin.

Since she already knew he didn't respond well to direct questions about his past, she tried to slip one past him disguised as an offhand comment. ''I bet you were a business major in college.''

His hands stilled for only a moment and then he returned to his task. ''Why do you say that?''

"Just a guess. Am I right?"

"What makes you think I even went to college?"

"It's obvious that you're well educated. Did you go to a university in Texas?"

"I've taken a few classes here and there. Nothing particularly useful—like fence mending. I could use a class in that right now," he commented ruefully, studying his purpling thumb.

The guy was a master of answering questions without actually saying anything. Lindsey had been quite indignant when she'd told Serena about Sam's refusal to even consider an interview for the newspaper. "You really don't like to talk about yourself, do you?"

Examining the fence for more problem areas, Sam shrugged without meeting her eyes. "Not much to talk about."

She tagged after him as he moved away. "Somehow I find that hard to believe. Someone who's traveled as much as you have must have some interesting stories to tell."

"Not really." He pulled a weed from between two fence boards and tossed it over to the other side.

"Have you ever been married?"

"No. Have you?"

"No."

He tested a loose board, then pulled a nail from the pocket of his jeans. "Why not?"

"I just haven't met anyone who—wait a minute, I was asking *you* questions."

"I thought I'd answered them all."

"Hardly. Don't you have any long-term goals? Any plans for your future?"

"At the moment, my goal is to finish repairing this fence."

"That isn't what I meant, and you know it."

He straightened away from the fence. "That's the last loose board I could find. I don't think Walter will be getting out again any time soon."

"I'm thinking of finding Walter another home. I really don't have time to give him the attention he needs, and neither does Mother. He was Kara's dog, but she dumped him on us when she ran off with Pierce."

"He's a nice dog. Doesn't seem like much trouble, except for his curiosity to explore—for which I'm grateful, by the way. If it hadn't been for Walter, who knows how long I'd have lain in that ditch?"

"Okay, he's a great dog. You want him?"

Sam chuckled. "I think I'd better pass. I don't think my life would suit Walter."

"Living on the road, you mean."

He only shrugged again.

Serena was right on his heels as he carried the tools to the garage. "You're already thinking about moving on?"

"You're the one who said I should be making plans for the future."

That wasn't exactly what she'd had in mind. She tried to convince herself that she was reluctant to picture Sam walking away because she hated to see anyone with so much potential waste his life. It certainly wasn't for her sake. Like Walter, Sam tended to clutter up her comfortably predictable routines. She didn't have time for either of them.

"So, what do you do for fun on a Saturday night in Edstown?" Sam asked, wiping his hands on his jeans.

"Drive to a bigger town," she answered dryly.

"Little Rock's only an hour and a half away. Most folks go there for excitement."

"There's nothing at all to do here?"

She deliberated. "There's usually a Little League game at the ballpark. A group of guys gather at the pizza parlor to watch wrestling on the big-screen TV there. My mother and some of her friends get together every Saturday evening to play a dominoes game they call chicken scratch. Some teenagers park down by the lake to sneak beers and make out until Dan goes by to break it up and send them home."

"Do *you* have any plans for this evening?"

"Actually, I have some paperwork to tackle."

"That's no fun. Why don't you and I find something to do together? What'll it be, wrestling at the pizza parlor or parking at the lake?"

His cheerfully irreverent question made her eyebrows rise. "I beg your pardon?"

"If it's up to me, I'd choose the latter, of course," he added. "Except for the part about Dan Meadows sending us home. He already considers me trouble waiting to happen."

The image of her and Sam making out in a car like a couple of hormone-flooded teenagers should have been ridiculous. Instead, it ignited a heat inside her that was reflected in the warmth on her cheeks. "Don't be silly."

"Surely we can come up with something more interesting than you doing paperwork and me watching TV."

Even though she knew he was teasing her—at least she thought he was—Serena suddenly gave in to a rare, mischievous impulse. "As a matter of fact, we can. Meet me at my car at seven. And bring an appetite.''

His smile turned quizzical. ''That sounds interesting.''

''Don't be late,'' she added lightly, even as a part of her wondered what on earth she was doing.

''Yes, ma'am.''

Sam was chuckling when they separated. Serena was wondering if she had finally lost her mind.

As they'd agreed, Sam was waiting by Serena's car at seven o'clock. His limited wardrobe didn't provide many options, but he wore freshly washed jeans with his denim shirt. He assumed they weren't going anywhere fancy, since Serena knew exactly what was in his closet.

He had his answer when she joined him wearing jeans and a thin red peasant-style blouse. Obviously a casual evening was in store for them. Though he was mildly curious, he didn't really care what she had planned. The prospect of spending the evening with her was intriguing enough in itself.

Not that he was expecting anything other than a couple of hours of companionship and diversion, he assured himself. No matter how attractive he found this woman—and she did look fine in her jeans—she was still off-limits to him. At least until he knew for sure there was no significant barrier between them.

''So where are we going?'' he asked, more to distract himself than because he really cared.

''I've decided to surprise you,'' she said as she opened the driver's door of her car.

He couldn't resist the impulse to flash her a wolfish

grin when he slid into the passenger's seat. "Sounds promising."

Fastening her seat belt, she sighed. "Are you going to spend the entire evening talking in innuendos?"

He chuckled. "That would be tiresome of me, wouldn't it?"

"It certainly would."

"Then I'll try to confine myself to only an occasional innuendo."

"I'd appreciate that," she said and started the car.

Amused by her wry tone, he snapped his safety belt into place and sprawled back in the seat, content to let her take him where she wanted.

She drove through the now familiar downtown section and beneath an overpass into a part of town Sam hadn't seen before. The houses here weren't as nice as the ones in Serena's neighborhood, and the yards were small and haphazardly landscaped. She drove past a used-car lot filled with vehicles only one step above the junkyard, and then a boarded-up former convenience store. After bumping over tracks that hadn't seen a train in years, she turned into a parking lot almost filled with pickups, sport utility vehicles and aging sedans. A neon sign above the door of the rough-sided building said Gaylord's.

Tilting his head, Sam studied the place. "A honky-tonk?"

Serena shrugged. "Honky-tonk. Dive. Dump. Call it whatever you want, the food's good."

"I wouldn't have thought this was your sort of place."

"I've grown rather fond of it because I have to keep coming here to find Marvin—the managing editor of the paper. If my lecture to him paid off the other day,

I guess I'll have to find another excuse to pop in every so often."

"Looks like I'm your excuse tonight."

"You'll do. Let's go."

Amused again by her brusque tone, he reached for the door handle. "Most flattering offer I've had in days."

The inside of Gaylord's looked very much the way Sam had expected, judging from the outside. Dim lights, crowded-together tables, a long bar at one end where solitary drinkers hunched over mugs and shot glasses. Zydeco music played from high-mounted speakers, and the decorations, such as they were, seemed meant to resemble Mardi Gras.

He'd been in places like this before, he realized abruptly—many of them. He felt oddly at home here in a way he hadn't in the tidy diner or on the sidewalks of downtown Edstown.

"Hey, Serena. Marvin's not here tonight."

Serena nodded to the portly man who'd greeted her from behind the bar. "I'm not looking for Marvin tonight, Chuck. I've brought a friend to taste your gumbo."

Chuck's florid face creased with a broad grin. "He's in for a treat, yeah? Find yourselves a seat and I'll send someone over to you."

"We'll be in the nonsmoking section."

Chuck laughed. "We'll find you there for sure."

Motioning for Sam to follow, Serena led the way across the large, smoke-filled room to a somewhat secluded table in the back corner.

"This is the nonsmoking section?" Sam asked as he held her seat for her.

"This and the table on either side. I've been trying

to convince Chuck to section off a bigger area that actually *is* smoke free, but he's strongly resistant to any sort of change.''

The scents of smoke and beer swirled around them, tugging again at Sam's memories. One of the articles he'd read at the library had mentioned that the sense of smell was a powerful cue to memory. So was the sense of taste, he discovered when he took a sip of the beer a waitress set in front of him a few minutes later.

He'd ordered beer because Serena had told him that was what the regulars usually drank here, though she had declined anything but water. The taste didn't stir specific memories in him, but rather a jumble of confused emotions. He couldn't say they were good feelings—something about the taste of the beer on his tongue was rather too familiar and somewhat depressing. He had a vague image of himself sitting alone in a darkened room, drinking beer from a can, a TV flickering in front of him.

Setting the mug down so abruptly the beverage sloshed perilously close to the brim, he strained to fill in the details of the cheerless recollection. *Any* details. He felt as if he was getting a little closer—and then Serena spoke, bringing him suddenly back to the present.

''Sam? Is something wrong with your beer?''

He focused on her face. She looked concerned, making him wonder how long he'd been sitting there staring into his mug. ''It's fine. I'm not much of a beer drinker, I guess,'' he said, pushing the mug aside.

''Neither am I. But I thought most men liked it.''

''That's what you get for thinking,'' he drawled as he pushed the now-distant semi-memory to the back of his mind. Maybe it would come back to him later if he didn't push it. "You said you recommend the gumbo?"

"Definitely. The crawfish étouffée and po'boy sandwiches are good, too. Chuck moved here from Baton Rouge, and his Cajun recipes are authentic."

He couldn't remember if he'd ever had Cajun food, but it sounded good. "Why don't you order for us, since you know the menu so well?"

While Serena gave their order to a teenager who bore a strong resemblance to the man behind the bar, Sam glanced at the other customers. It was a casual gathering, with jeans, T-shirts and shorts the attire of choice. Many of the men, and a few of the women, wore ball caps they hadn't bothered to remove upon entering. He spotted several tattooed arms and a few other ink-injected body parts, but the crowd was generally well-behaved. Maybe because it was still early and the serious partying hadn't begun yet, he thought as a noisy group of three women and two men entered and claimed a central table.

A man Sam recognized as a regular breakfast customer from the diner approached the table and slapped him on the shoulder. "Yo, Sam. Is Serena giving you a taste of the Edstown hot spots?"

"Hi, Bill. Sam asked me what there was to do here on a Saturday night," Serena answered with a smile. "So I'm showing him."

"This is pretty much it," Bill said to Sam with a grin. "Unless you want to join the kids over at the pizza parlor watching wrestling."

"I've heard there's some action down at the lake on Saturday evenings."

Bill laughed and thumped Sam's shoulder again. "There's that, too. I used to go down there with my girlfriends in high school. Can't tell you how many times old Chief Ferrell tapped on steamy windows and made us move on.''

''That's an Edstown tradition Sam's just going to have to miss—at least tonight,'' Serena said primly.

Her statement elicited a belly laugh from Bill, along with another punch on Sam's shoulder. ''Can't blame a guy for trying, right, buddy? Especially when you're out with a girl as pretty as Serena.''

Before Sam could answer, Serena said gruffly, ''I think your wife is getting bored, Bill. Maybe you'd better get back to her—before you wedge your foot any deeper in your mouth.''

Cheerful as always, Bill nodded. ''I get you, Serena. You want me to disappear and leave you two to your dinner. I'll see you at the diner, Sam. Keep the coffee hot for me.''

''I'll do that,'' Sam replied, surreptitiously rubbing his shoulder. The older man ambled off, stopping to gossip at another table, leaving his wife alone for a while longer. ''Nice guy, but he really packs a wallop.''

Serena gave him a sympathetic smile. ''A few new bruises?''

''Very likely. But at least these were given in a spirit of friendship.''

Her smile faded. ''Do you think the men who beat you up will ever be found?''

A twinge of familiar guilt made him avoid her eyes. ''It doesn't look likely.''

''You said you were traveling with them? Surely you know their names—something that might lead the authorities to them.''

''I wasn't traveling with them. I'd simply accepted

a ride from them. I don't know anything useful about them.'' He was really tired of the lie, especially with Serena, but this was neither the time nor the place to level with her.

He was relieved when the waiter set steaming bowls of gumbo in front of them, interrupting the conversation. The spicy soup was thick with seafood and vegetables, served over a bed of fluffy rice. He scooped up a spoonful of shrimp, okra and tomatoes. ''Man, that's good,'' he murmured, savoring the taste.

Serena had watched him take the bite as if curious about his reaction. ''You don't think it's too hot? Some people think Chuck's gumbo is too spicy the first time they taste it.''

Swallowing a second spoonful, Sam grinned. ''Hot? Lady, I've had chili that makes this stuff taste like…ice cream.'' He stumbled over the last words, suddenly aware of how easily they had come to him. He could almost smell that mouth-scalding chili he'd alluded to—but he couldn't for the life of him remember where he'd eaten it, or with whom.

Serena didn't seem to notice his momentary hesitation. ''You Texans are always bragging about your chili.''

Texan. Serena seemed convinced that was his background. Maybe she was right. He certainly wasn't going to argue with her. He spent the next few minutes concentrating on his gumbo, listening to the music and mentally chasing after that elusive glimmer of memory.

He couldn't capture it.

The efficient young waiter cleared away their empty gumbo bowls and replaced them with their next course—crawfish étouffée for Sam and a shrimp po'boy for Serena. Again, the food was spicy, but enjoyably so. They took time to savor it. As the evening advanced, the place became crowded with customers shoulder-to-shoulder at the bar where they waited for tables. Drinks flowed freely, and both the music and the crowd seemed to grow louder. Eruptions of loud laughter became common, from deep guffaws to shrill giggles. As comfortable as he felt there, Sam still thought Serena was out of place; she seemed more the tearoom or French restaurant type than a Cajun honky-tonk regular.

It was almost impossible to keep a conversation going in a normal tone. Sam and Serena made a couple of attempts, but for the most part focused on their dinners. They were almost finished when Chuck wandered over from the bar. His booming voice carried easily over the noise. "How's that food, eh?"

Sam set his fork on his empty plate. "It was excellent. I enjoyed every bite."

"Not too spicy?"

"Just spicy enough," Sam assured him.

Chuck grinned in approval and thumped Sam's shoulder. "I like your friend, Serena. You bring him back any time, you hear?"

"Next time, I'm wearing body armor," Sam muttered, rubbing his shoulder as Chuck moved on to the next table.

"I'm sorry." Serena leaned closer. "I didn't hear what you said."

"Never mind. Do you want dessert?"

"No, I'm too full."

"So am I." He motioned for the waiter to bring the check.

"You're my guest tonight," Serena said. "I'm buying."

"No, you're not." He hoped his firm tone made it clear he didn't want any argument about this.

He should have known Serena better than that. "I'm the one who brought you here," she said. "I will pick up the tab."

He'd had all the charity he intended to take. It was time to reassert his independence. He'd been paid after the lunch shift that day; he could take care of this modestly priced meal and put most of the rest toward his debts. "I'm paying."

This time his determination seemed to get through. "At least let me pay for my own," she said.

Wearing a patient smile, he spoke evenly. "Serena, I don't lose my temper very often—I can't even recall the last time I did so—but you're pushing my buttons. I would like to pay for our dinner this evening."

She subsided with a grumbled, "Damned male ego."

"Exactly."

"Just don't think paying for my meal is going to get you a trip to the lake this evening."

He had to laugh at that. "Like the man said, you can't blame a guy for trying."

Feeling oddly pleased with himself, he paid the waiter. After leaving a tip on the table, he accompanied Serena out of the restaurant, dodging tipsy customers and stopping a couple of times to greet acquaintances—mostly Serena's, but a few people who recognized him from his first week at the diner. Finally outside, they took a moment to relish the relative quiet of the parking lot.

"I enjoyed the meal," Sam said after a moment,

then winced when he realized he'd spoken a bit too loudly.

Serena smiled. "It takes a few minutes to adjust, doesn't it? It's a wonder Chuck has any hearing left at all after being exposed to that every night."

Speaking in his normal voice, Sam asked as they walked to the car, "So this is an average Saturday evening for you?"

"Hardly," she answered ruefully, unlocking the doors. "This is the first time in months I've taken an evening to just hang out and do nothing productive. I'm usually in meetings, either with clients or newspaper employees. Or I'm trying to catch up on the newspaper business details that pile up while I'm taking care of my legal practice—or vice versa. Or I'm answering e-mail or phone messages or doing research or writing briefs or..."

"I get the picture." He slid into the passenger's seat and buckled the seat belt. "You know what they say about all work and no play."

Starting the engine, she answered, "It pays the bills."

This was not the voice of a woman who was entirely content with her life, Sam realized, studying her profile as she drove out of the parking lot. She was going through the motions, successfully keeping up with the details, but there was a hole in her life that she hadn't been able to fill to her complete satisfaction.

That feeling was as familiar to him as the scent of beer and cigarettes had been earlier. And just as frustratingly elusive. He knew it well—but he didn't know why.

He could make himself crazy at this rate—if he wasn't already there.

Chapter Eight

Serena had to pull over to allow a fire truck to pass on the way home. Both she and Sam watched as the aging emergency vehicle sped past, lights flashing and siren wailing, then turned at the next intersection. "I hope that isn't a serious emergency," she murmured, resisting a voyeuristic impulse to follow.

"Sirens—not a sound you hear very often around here," Sam commented.

"You won't hear me complaining about that."

"No desire at all for the fast-paced life of a big city?"

"I'll leave the fast lane to my sister. My life is here."

"Your mother worries about you, you know."

She shot him a look, wondering just how much her chatty mother had said to him. "In what way?"

"She's afraid you're getting into a rut. Working too

hard, playing too little. She said there are very few single people your age here, and she worries about your social life."

"She's more worried about her lack of grandchildren," Serena answered dryly. "She's the only non-grandmother in her Saturday-night dominoes group, as she loves to remind me every Sunday morning."

Sam chuckled. "So how come you aren't making an effort to help her out with that?" he teased.

"That takes two," she answered with a shrug intended to disguise her sudden self-consciousness. "I haven't found anyone I want to mix genes with. And besides, I'm not sure I'm cut out for motherhood. I'm having enough trouble being responsible for Kara's dog."

He laughed again. "Now you're selling yourself short."

She'd had enough of that subject, especially with this man. "You know, maybe I *would* like dessert. How does a snow cone sound to you?"

"A snow cone," he repeated in a neutral tone that made it sound as if he'd never heard the term before. "Sounds great."

She turned left on North Street, heading for Patty's Polar Ice Shack, a concessions trailer that operated during summer months on a vacant lot next to the local discount store. "What's your favorite flavor?"

"It's, uh, been so long since I had one that I hardly remember. What's yours?"

"Wild cherry. Sometimes I order grape. Mom always chooses orange. Kara used to try something different every time—offbeat flavors like tiger's blood and ocean breeze and wedding cake."

"Your sister's always had a taste for adventure?"

Serena wrinkled her nose. "I wish she had confined it to snow cone flavors."

"You wouldn't really want her to stay here if she was unhappy, would you, just because she felt obligated to run the newspaper to keep your mother and you happy?"

Serena felt herself getting defensive again—as she always did when she and Sam discussed Kara. She wished she could make him understand that her irritation with her sister was based on genuine concern. Kara was destined—at least in Serena's opinion—to end up heartbroken, penniless, disillusioned—all the things that happened to a woman who totally immersed herself in a man. She'd seen it all too many times in her law practice—women stripped of their confidence, their dignity, their savings, all because they'd trusted the wrong men. As far as Serena was concerned, Kara simply hadn't known Pierce long enough to be sure he wasn't using her.

Besides, she thought with a ripple of sadness as she parked in front of the concessions trailer, she missed her sister.

"I'll have the wild cherry tonight," she said, deciding to leave Sam's questions about Kara unanswered. "What will you have?"

Sam studied the illuminated sign listing a dismayingly long list of flavors. "Bubble gum?" he asked quizzically.

She shuddered. "I have a feeling that flavor would be sweet enough to induce a coma in anyone over twelve."

"I think I'll have grape."

"Nice, safe choice."

"That's me," he said with a smile. "Just a dull, safe-type guy."

It was a good thing she wasn't eating anything at that moment, Serena thought wryly. She very well might have choked.

Several picnic tables had been set up for customers, shaded with colorful umbrellas for daytime and decorated with strings of colored lights after dark. A teenage girl in the cramped metal trailer took their orders from a pass-through window at one end, then heaped finely shaved ice into cone-shaped paper cups and poured on syrup in the flavors they had requested. They carried the dripping treats to the only empty picnic table. The other tables were occupied by families, syrup-smeared children chattering and giggling and jostling each other, one boy complaining loudly that his sister's cone had more syrup than his.

"Well, this is quite a contrast to our first stop of the evening," Sam commented, eyeing his grape snow cone as if he wasn't quite sure how to begin eating it.

"Hey, you wanted to experience Saturday night in Edstown."

Sam took a tentative nibble of grape-flavored ice. "Not bad. Pretty sweet, though."

"Extremely sweet," Serena agreed, licking wild cherry syrup off her lower lip. "Haven't you ever had one of these?"

"Sure. I mean, I must have, right?"

She studied him for a moment over her dessert. "Sometimes you say the oddest things."

His smile was lopsided. "You think so?"

"And then you do that."

Imitating a boy at the next table, he drank syrup out of the rim of his snow cone cup. "Do what?"

"Deflect my questions with another question or a smart comment."

"Do I?"

She sighed and took a crunching bite of ice.

"Serena, hi!" Holding a bright green snow cone, Lindsey Gray slid onto the bench beside Serena and nodded to her companion. "Mr. Wallace."

"Ms. Gray," he responded gravely. "A pleasure to see you again."

"It's a bit ridiculous to be so formal over snow cones," Serena said with a roll of her eyes. "First names, okay? Sam, meet Lindsey."

Sam's lips twitched. "I believe Ms. Gray is still annoyed with me for turning down an interview."

"I'm not annoyed, Sam," she replied equably. "I still wish you'd agreed, of course, but I don't hold grudges."

"I'm glad to hear that."

Serena looked at her employee. "How did things go at the paper today?"

"Well..."

"Never mind." Wincing in response to the reporter's tone, Serena shook her head. "Maybe I don't want to know."

"You really are going to have to do something about Marvin, you know. The paper can't keep operating this way much longer."

"I'll do something soon. You and Riley just try to keep things going a little longer, okay?"

"I'm trying. And so is Riley, in his own way. But we really need an editor we can depend on."

"I'll talk to Marvin again."

"Like that will do any good. Face it, Serena, it's

not going to get any better. Marvin needs treatment, not lectures.''

Serena tossed the melting remains of her dessert into a nearby trash can, wiped her hands on a paper napkin and then rubbed her temples with her fingertips. "I know that. But I can't force him to get help.''

"And you're too softhearted to fire him because you don't want him to end up in a gutter or something.'' Lindsey gave Sam a look filled with irony. "Can you believe it? A tenderhearted lawyer. Bet you didn't know such a critter existed, hmm?''

"Now *that* seems like a headline for your newspaper,'' Sam said.

"Nah. Old news. Everyone knows Serena's not as tough as she pretends to be.''

Uncomfortable at the direction the conversation was taking, Serena changed the subject. "We passed a fire truck on the way over. It looked like it was responding to an emergency call.''

"I already know about that. Riley just called and said he's covering it. He heard the details on his scanner. The old dairy barn on Locust Street caught fire.''

"That building's been abandoned for several years. That's somewhat of a relief. I was afraid someone's house was burning.''

"You can read all about it in tomorrow's *Evening Star*. It'll be front-page news—right above a photo of the winner of tonight's chicken-scratch game.'' Lindsey spoke dryly to Sam. "As you can see, there isn't a lot of hard news to report around here. That's why I was so interested in the stranger found all beaten up in a ditch.''

"Lindsey.'' Even for the compulsively irreverent

reporter, that comment seemed a little too flip to Serena.

Sam seemed to find it more amusing than offensive. "Sorry I ruined your chance at a big byline."

Lindsey shrugged matter-of-factly. "It's not like I have a lot of competition. I get all the bylines I want."

"So why aren't you chasing stories in a bigger market? Some place where a dominoes game isn't front-page news?"

Serena glared at Sam. "Please don't try to deprive me of my one truly dependable employee. Talk Lindsey into leaving, and I might as well put the paper to bed for good right now."

"You know I'm not going anywhere for a while," Lindsey replied. Glancing at Sam, she added, "I used to work in Little Rock, but I moved here a couple of years ago. My father's in poor health and my brother is career military, so he doesn't get home very often. I'll stay as long as Dad needs me."

As different as Serena and Lindsey were in many ways, they both placed their obligations to their families above their own desires. Serena wondered if Sam had made note of that—and, considering his defense of Kara, how he felt about it. Not that she cared all that much about what he thought, of course.

Lindsey finished her treat and tossed the empty cup into the trash can. "I think I'll run by the old dairy barn and see if there's anything interesting going on. I just had a craving for a lime snow cone on the way. I'll see you guys around."

"You still haven't stopped by the diner for that cup of coffee I offered," Sam reminded Lindsey as she stood.

She gave him a dimpled smile. "I might just take you up on that invitation soon."

Realizing that she was frowning, Serena quickly smoothed her expression. It was certainly none of her concern if Sam wanted to flirt with Lindsey—or if she flirted in return. The only reason Serena disapproved was that they really didn't know this guy very well. He was several years older than Lindsey and an admitted drifter—but undeniably good-looking and charming. She would hate to see her star reporter swept off her feet when there was no future in it.

With her father ill and her workplace in turmoil, Lindsey could be vulnerable—especially if Serena was right about her harboring an unrequited crush on Dan. She would hate to see Lindsey hurt—which was the *only* reason she cared if Sam flirted with her, she assured herself.

She was in a rather pensive mood when she parked in her garage a little while later. Her mother wasn't home yet; it was only ten o'clock and the dominoes games often went on until eleven. Serena frequently teased her mother about having the more exciting social life.

After tonight, Sam probably thought Serena was just about the dullest woman under sixty he'd ever spent an evening with.

Apparently, he wasn't much of a mind reader. "I had a great time tonight."

"I'm sure you've had more exciting evenings."

"Not recently." He opened his door.

Serena could have entered her house directly from the garage, but instead she found herself following Sam onto the walkway that led past the swing and rose garden to the guest house. "Mother and I usually go to church on Sunday mornings. I don't know if you're interested, but you're welcome to join us tomorrow if you'd like.''

"Your mother already invited me. I think I'll pass this time."

She wasn't really surprised. "Sure. So, I'll see you around then."

"You bet. Thanks again for going with me this evening. It was a nice change of pace."

"For me, too," she admitted, oddly reluctant for the evening to end.

A moth fluttered out of the shadows and tangled in Serena's hair. Sam reached out to gently disengage it, setting it free to fly toward the closest light. The move brought them closer, and he didn't immediately step away. He combed his fingers through her hair again. "I like the way you wear your hair. Soft. Natural."

Now he was flirting with *her*. And she wouldn't let herself be carried away by it for the same reasons she'd mentally listed for Lindsey—this was not a man to start depending on. But it was rather nice to stand in the moonlight with him, the scent of roses in the night air, his fingers brushing her cheek. Even a level-headed, practical woman like Serena could appreciate the romance of the situation.

If this had been a real date, a good-night kiss would be appropriate. A light brush of lips or even a more lingering exploration—neither would have been out of line. Had this been a real date, of course.

She realized that Sam was looking at her mouth, as if similar thoughts were playing through his mind. The possibility that he was thinking about kissing her made her mouth tingle as if their lips had already touched. There was a certain allure in the idea of kissing an attractive stranger—a tempting element of risk in knowing so little about him, having so little reassurance that he was safe. She felt herself swaying toward him and sensed that he was moving toward her, as well.

She was the one who put up a hand, resting it on his chest to hold him away. Kara had the taste for adventure in this family, not Serena. The only wild taste Serena indulged was her preference for wild cherry snow cones. "This isn't a good idea."

"No," he murmured. "Probably not." But he didn't move away—and neither did Serena.

"All we shared was dinner and a snow cone."

"Right. Just a friendly dinner." His lips had quirked into a half-smile that made her even more tempted to taste them. Just a taste...

He must have read the impulse in her eyes. Once again, he leaned his head closer—and this time she didn't move away.

It wasn't a long kiss—but it certainly was a powerful one. The glimpse it gave her of what could be between them if she wasn't careful shook her to her toenails. Her hands weren't quite steady when he released her, and she didn't trust her voice to reply steadily when he murmured, "Good night, Serena."

Without a word, she turned and headed quickly toward the house. It really didn't matter if he found her retreat amusing. She needed some distance from him.

She might as well tackle some of that paperwork tonight, after all, she thought as she closed herself into her house. She didn't think she'd be able to sleep for a while, anyway.

Sam stood in the darkened bedroom of the guest house, staring at the light burning in an upstairs window of the main house. Serena's room, he presumed. It was after midnight, and she was still awake. Her mother had come home almost an hour ago, and because he saw no other lights he assumed Marjorie had already turned in. But Serena was still awake. Working? Or—like him—was she spending the evening replaying the time they'd spent together? Remembering the brief kiss they'd shared in the rose garden.

She'd been right to run. He'd like to think he'd have had the sense to stop with that one kiss if she hadn't, but he couldn't offer any guarantees in that respect. After all, he'd wanted to kiss her all evening. And she had thought about kissing him, too. He'd seen it in her eyes.

Now what was he going to do?

Sam was surprised to answer a knock on his door Sunday afternoon and find the police chief on the other side. "What have I done?"

Dan smiled wryly. "Automatic assumption or guilty conscience?"

"Assumption. As far as I know, I haven't broken any laws."

"Then there's no need for me to haul you in, I guess. How about if we go fishing, instead?"

"Fishing?" Sam felt both his eyebrows rise. "You're kidding, right?"

"Nope. I've got the afternoon off and I'm in the mood to catch some fish. I thought you might like to go with me."

"Why me?"

Dan's grin deepened. "Everyone else I asked was busy."

Chuckling, Sam nodded. "Now I understand."

"So…you want to go?"

"Sure. But I don't have any fishing gear."

"Already covered. Got a cap?"

"Not even that."

"I've got an extra in the truck. Let's go."

Half an hour later, Sam found himself in a flat-bottomed fishing boat with the chief of police, a borrowed cap on his head, a fishing license purchased from a bait shop tucked into his shirt pocket. He'd done this before, he decided as he cast toward a promising-looking hole—sat in a boat with another guy, listening to the water lapping against the sides, inhaling the slightly fishy smell of lake water and the faint, gassy fumes from the outboard motor. He could almost picture the man who usually sat in the other end of the boat—brown hair, deeply tanned skin, someone he knew well. Like a brother.

Was he a brother? A longtime friend? Or just a figment of his erratic imagination?

"Nice cast," Dan observed. "You do a lot of fishing?"

"Some. You?"

"Every chance I get."

"I guess you stay pretty busy with your job. You're on call around the clock, aren't you?"

"Pretty much." Dan glanced ruefully at the pager clipped to his belt. "And, yeah, the job keeps me running. We don't have a lot of crimes around here—haven't had a murder in four years, and that was a domestic abuse case out on the edge of town—but we have our share of Saturday night brawls and break-ins. Unfortunately, the days of leaving doors unlocked are over, even in small towns like this one."

"Did you ever arrest anyone for the break-ins last week?"

"No," Dan grumbled. "I'm pretty sure I've got three, maybe four burglaries committed by the same people, but I haven't found anything to lead me to them. Yet. I will, though. They get cocky when they think they've gotten away with a few, and then they get sloppy. That's when I catch them."

"What about the kid I met the other day? The one with the bruise on his face?"

"Zach Hinson." Dan's brows dipped into a frown. "Yeah, I checked on him later that day. His mother swore he fell off a skateboard. Her live-in boyfriend told the same story."

"And the boy?"

Dan shrugged and reeled in his lure. "He didn't dispute their story."

"Did you believe them?"

From beneath the brim of his cap, Dan's eyes met Sam's. "No."

Sam sighed. "But there's nothing you can do without proof."

"Not a damned thing."

Sam remembered the flashes of disturbing memories he'd experienced while he'd talked to young Zach. The feeling that he'd identified a bit too well with the frightened, probably mistreated boy. It bugged him that the few memories that had come back to him were so sketchy and hazy. Being slapped as a kid. Dining in an elegant restaurant. Drinking beer in a smoky club. Fishing with a buddy. The vague images were no more real or substantial to him than scenes recalled from TV or movies. Was that all they were? How could he tell the difference between imagination and rcality when he had no frame of reference with which to distinguish them?

Dan seemed to think Sam's silence carried an implied criticism. "I'm not turning my back on the kid, Sam. I'll be keeping a close eye on them. First evidence I have that either the mother or her jerk boyfriend is mistreating that kid, I'll move in so fast their heads will spin."

"I'm sure you will. It just makes me sick to think of anyone hitting a little kid."

"I hear you. But there's very little I can do without proof. Maybe it'll help some that I went by to talk to them. I think I made it clear that I'm keeping an eye on them."

"Sometimes that's enough," Sam agreed. "At least, it should be—"

His words broke off when he felt a sudden tug on his line. He moved to set the hook, then swore softly beneath his breath. "Missed it."

Looking away from his own line for a minute, Dan opened the small ice chest he'd brought along. "Are you thirsty?"

The thought of drinking beer still made Sam's stomach tighten in protest. "What do you have?"

"Cola or grape soda."

Relieved, Sam accepted a grape soda. The sweet taste lingered in his mouth, reminding him of the snow cone he'd eaten during his outing with Serena. Dan caught a nice-size bass then, which kept him busy and Sam entertained for a few minutes, and then they fell back into companionable silence again while they waited for the fish to bite.

Sam broke the silence. "I heard you had some excitement late yesterday. A fire on Locust Street?"

"Yeah. An old dairy barn burned. The fire almost got out of control and threatened a couple of homes nearby, but the fire department managed to contain it in time. How did you hear about it?"

"Serena and I ran into Lindsey last night. She told us about the fire and said she was going there when she left us."

As Sam had noticed before, Dan reacted visibly at the mention of the reporter's name. He scowled. "Yeah, she showed up. Got under everybody's feet asking questions and wanting to know what we were doing and why. The fire chief was about ready to tie her up with a fire hose before his job was finished."

Amused, Sam commented, "I thought the other reporter was covering the fire."

"Yeah, Riley was there—standing quietly out of the way observing the action, as Lindsey should have been doing."

"She seems very...dedicated."

"She's a pain in the butt," Dan answered bluntly. "Her brother was my best friend in school, and Lindsey's always been a decent kid, but when she gets in her reporter mode, she's like a pit bull with a juicy bone."

"You think of her as a kid?" Sam pictured the attractive redhead, remembering sleek curves and intelligent eyes. She was young, maybe, but hardly a kid.

"Habit," Dan admitted. "Like I said, she was my best friend's little sister. Quite a bit younger than us. I guess that's still the way I think of her at times."

Sam had a feeling Lindsey wouldn't be flattered. She seemed so determined to be taken seriously.

"The fire chief thinks the fire was deliberately set,"

Dan commented, his gaze on the water where he worked his lure.

"Arson?"

"Yeah. The signs are definitely there."

"Insurance scam?"

"No. The barn's been vacant for years. The owner let the insurance lapse some time ago."

"Maybe an accident? A trespasser who let a fire get out of hand?"

"Maybe. But it looks like someone meant to burn the place down."

"I hope it doesn't—hey." Responding to another tug on his line, Sam swiftly lifted the tip of his rod to set the hook. The line zinged as the fish sped away from the boat.

"Looks like you've got a big one."

"He's a fighter, that's for sure."

Dan seemed prepared to watch the battle, but was quickly distracted by a strike on his own lure. That ended any serious conversation for a while. The rest of the afternoon passed quickly and pleasantly, making Sam glad everyone else had been busy when the police chief had been in the mood to fish. It sure beat sitting around the tiny guest house mooning over Serena, he told himself with a grimace.

Sam was working in the yard when Serena arrived home from work on the following Friday. The grass was freshly mowed, and he was running a weed trimmer around the fence. It was still quite hot, even though the sun was dipping close to the horizon. Sam's T-shirt, wet with sweat, clung to his skin. He'd ditched the wrist brace a few days earlier, and his arms looked strong and muscular. From beneath the cap that shaded his face from the late afternoon sun, his hair hung damply around his face, and there was a streak of dirt on one cheek.

Serena felt her mouth go dry.

Seeing her watching him, he turned off the noisy machine. She felt a need to fill the sudden silence. "Hi."

He wiped the back of one wrist across his forehead. "Hi. How was your day?"

"Long. The yard looks great. You worked hard."

He shrugged. "Marjorie said she wasn't happy with the lawn service she hired last time, so I told her I'd take care of it until she found someone else."

"You don't have to do this, you know."

"We've had this conversation before." He hefted the weed trimmer over his shoulder. "I'll put this back in the garage."

Since it was obvious there was no need to try again to convince him that he didn't have to repay every debt immediately—and obvious that he had recovered amazingly well from the injuries he'd sustained only two weeks earlier—she changed the subject as she followed him into the garage. They hadn't had much chance to talk during the past few days. She'd been extremely busy with her law practice and the newspaper business—or at least that's what she'd told herself while she avoided him long enough to recover from a brief kiss that had nearly knocked her for a loop. "That's the cap Dan gave you when you went fishing Sunday, isn't it?"

"Yeah. He insisted I keep it."

"To be honest, I was rather surprised to hear that he invited you."

"So was I." Sam set the weed trimmer in its rack. "He said everyone else was busy."

"I think he's starting to like you."

"Oh, I wouldn't go that far."

"Don't you think there's a chance you and Dan could become friends?"

"I certainly wouldn't want the chief of police for an enemy."

He was being even more exasperatingly uncommunicative than usual. Maybe he was tired, or maybe he was making sure there was no repeat of that kiss last Saturday night. Very wise of him, of course. It had to be as obvious to him as it was to her that it would be a mistake for them to get involved, even on a temporary basis. They could be friends, of course— but nothing more. And that was exactly the way it should be.

"I guess I'd better go in," she said, taking a step backward. "I have some things to—"

Her words ended in a gasp when the heel of her pump slid on a nail that had been lying unnoticed on the concrete floor, causing her ankle to twist sharply. She could have righted herself more quickly had she not been wearing a form-fitting straight skirt. She was convinced she was going to fall—but Sam caught her just in time.

"Are you all right?" he demanded, his hands on her forearms.

"Yes, I…" She grimaced, feeling incredibly stupid. "Just clumsy."

"I must have dropped that nail earlier," he said in chagrin. "It was damned careless of me. You could have been hurt."

"Don't worry about it. I should have watched where I stepped."

"Can you put your weight on your ankle?"

They both looked down as she tested it. Her ankle twinged, but she had no trouble standing on it. "It's fine, really. I just sort of fell off my shoe."

He relaxed enough to smile. "You women and your high heels."

"These aren't so high," she protested, glancing down again. "Only a couple of inches."

When she looked up, his mouth seemed suddenly closer to hers. "A couple of inches makes you just the right height," he murmured.

"For what?" she asked inanely.

His wicked smile, so close to her mouth, was answer in itself.

"Oh. Well." She swallowed, trying futilely to come up with a clever response. "I think we should..."

"Yes?" His bright blue eyes gleamed. She'd always thought of blue as a cool color—until now, when she saw just how warm blue could be.

"Um..." What was it she'd intended to say? "We shouldn't..."

"No," he murmured. "We shouldn't. But I'm having a real hard time remembering that right now."

"So am I," she admitted, needing no clarification of his obscure statement.

His hands still rested on her forearms, though she had fully regained her balance. She laid her hands against his chest, feeling the warmth of his skin through the damp T-shirt. Either one of them had only to move a couple of inches to bring their mouths together. They stood frozen there for several long moments, neither quite confident enough to make that move.

Serena knew she should step away and knew Sam would release her immediately if she did. But she found herself as reluctant to take that step away from him as she was afraid to make the move toward him.

Kara was the risk taker in the family, she reminded herself as she had the last time she and Sam had been this close to a kiss. Kara was the one who had boldly pursued the man who'd attracted her interest. Kara was the one who...

"Oh, the hell with it," she muttered, and reached up to press her mouth to Sam's.

It seemed that Kara wasn't the only Schaffer with an occasional desire to take a risk.

Chapter Nine

Kissing Serena was everything Sam had remembered it to be—and more. As he savored her warm, soft, moist mouth, he vaguely remembered other kisses. No names or faces, just fuzzy impressions. But he didn't know if any other kisses had made his pulse race like this, his head spin, his hands tremble. It had been this way the first time he'd kissed her, even though it had lasted barely longer than a heartbeat. Either he still hadn't fully recovered from his illness—or there was a powerful attraction between them.

He'd have bet on the latter.

Serena had taken him by surprise when she initiated this kiss, and she continued to overwhelm him with her responsiveness. Her lips parted, giving him better access to the taste of her. Intoxicating. Dangerously so. A little more and he would be tempted to ignore all the very good reasons they shouldn't be kissing in the first place.

Apparently, Serena's better judgment was similarly undermined by the embrace. Her hands crept upward, sliding around his neck, bringing her body more fully against his. The shock of contact brought him abruptly back to his senses.

He was sweaty, disheveled and dirty after a full day of work. Serena looked very much the successful young attorney in a trim suit and neat black pumps, her hair twisted at the back of her head, diamond studs in her ears. Anyone observing them would know at a glance that they were a mismatched pair. Sam was too vividly aware of all the complications that were *not* visible.

Like the not-so-insignificant fact that neither of them knew who the hell he was.

He lifted his head. Serena's eyelids were heavy, her cheeks flushed, her lips damp and reddened. She looked like a woman who'd just been thoroughly kissed and wouldn't mind being kissed again. Releasing her and backing away took every bit of willpower Sam could muster.

"We should definitely not do that," he said as if their conversation had not been interrupted.

He watched her regain her equilibrium. She blinked a couple of times, drew a shaky breath, squared her shoulders and lifted her chin. "You're right," she said, and her voice was admirably steady. "Definitely."

"Definitely." He was glad she'd agreed—or at least he should be. He had enough problems without this added complication. Once he got his memory back—well, who knew. Maybe things would be different then. And maybe she would hate him for lying to her from the first time he'd spoken to her.

"I need a shower," he said, turning away. *A cold one,* he added silently.

"I'll see you later, I guess."

"Sure. Later." He walked toward the exit with long, determined strides. He couldn't resist glancing back as he stepped outside. Unaware that he could see her, Serena sagged against the wall, fanning her face with one hand. For some crazy reason, he was cheered by that confirmation that she was just as shaken by their kiss as he was.

The Rainbow Café was closed on Wednesday, July fourth. Most downtown offices were closed for the Independence Day holiday, so business at the diner would have been light, anyway. Marjorie asserted that it was more important to her to allow her employees to spend the day with their families than to try to make money from the few customers they'd have served.

Marjorie told Sam that a big celebration was held every July fourth at the high school football field. "It's a big deal around here. We have barbecue and watermelon and entertainment. After dark, there's a fireworks display."

She invited him to attend the celebration with Serena and her. Lacking a reasonable excuse to decline, he accepted.

Carrying lawn chairs, they walked through the gates of the football stadium at seven, shoulder to shoulder with what seemed to Sam to be a mob of other revelers. Either Edstown was more populated than he'd realized or people came from all over the area to attend the Independence Day celebration.

His nose twitched as the scent of barbecue wafted toward them from the big grills set up in the end zone. Lines were already forming for the burgers, hot dogs, potato salad and cold pork and beans provided by local merchants. At another table, stacks of plump watermelons were being sliced for dessert, and huge tubs of ice held canned soft drinks.

"All of this is free to the public?" he asked Serena, raising his voice over the sound of a gospel quartet singing on a makeshift stage in the center of the field.

Looking remarkably cool and fresh in her shorts and T-shirt, considering that the air was still almost stiflingly hot, she nodded. "Yes. It's our one big, city-wide festivity. Most of the local businesses contribute, and we publish their names in the *Evening Star* several times to thank them. It's good PR for them, and a nice community service for the city."

Marjorie, coordinated as always in a brightly colored knit tunic and matching slacks, had been craning her head since they arrived, scanning the crowd. Her search ended at an open-sided awning that had been set up not far from the food, but within clear view of the stage. The awning seemed to Sam to be filled with gray-haired ladies and a few equally mature men. "You two have a good time," Marjorie said cheerfully, already moving toward the awning. "I'll catch you later."

"You're leaving us?" Sam asked, lifting an eyebrow.

"You kids don't want an old lady tagging after you all evening. I'm sure you'd rather find other young people. Go on, now. Have fun. Serena, be sure to introduce Sam to all your friends."

Serena rolled her eyes. "Yes, Mother."

Before Sam could say anything else, Marjorie had bustled away. "She does this every year," Serena said with a sigh. "Ditches me as soon as we get here. She says she doesn't want to cramp my style, but the truth is she likes to spend the evening gossiping with her friends. They giggle and whisper about everyone here—worse than any bunch of teenagers you've ever met."

"Aren't they going to eat? They don't look like they're in any hurry to get in line."

Serena's expression held both exasperation and reluctant admiration. "They don't have to get in line. They'll sit in their lawn chairs under the shade of that awning and pretty soon some solicitous teenagers, prodded by their mothers, will bring plates of food so the little old ladies don't have to exert themselves by standing in line in this heat."

Sam laughed. "As if Marjorie Schaffer isn't perfectly capable of carrying a plate of food."

"And so are most of her friends. But they're not above taking advantage of their years today. They love being treated with such deference."

Eyeing the lines waiting to be served, Sam asked, "So, how old does one have to be to qualify for that privilege?"

"Much older than we are," Serena replied with a smile. "Let's set these chairs down somewhere and get in line."

She'd been a bit stiff with him when they'd left her house a short while earlier. He didn't know whether it was their public surroundings or the deliberately casually friendly way he'd been treating her, but she was beginning to relax—and he was relieved. Both of them had had plenty of time to second-guess the impulsive kisses between them. He was certain she'd come to the same conclusion he had—the kisses had been a mistake. He would hate to see anything drive a wedge in the comfortable friendship that had been forming between them.

He needed the few friends he'd made here—at least until he remembered if he had any elsewhere.

As they waited in the long line for food, Sam idly scanned the crowd. He saw several people he'd met at the diner and the librarian he'd gotten to know as he'd researched amnesia articles and cruised the Internet for clues to his identity. He waved to her, and she waved back. Dan Meadows and a couple of his officers were highly visible, mingling, obviously on alert for signs of any trouble. Sam suspected that Dan would make very sure the annual Independence Day festivity proceeded smoothly, at least in the crowd control area.

He and Serena had almost reached the serving tables when Sam noticed a lone man wandering on the far side of the football field. Something about the guy struck him as odd. Maybe it was the way he was dressed—dark chinos, crisply pressed sport shirt, black oxfords, expensive sunglasses. He seemed out of place in the cutoffs-and-flip-flops crowd that had gathered in the summer heat. While everyone else was socializing, this man walked alone, exchanging only an occasional perfunctory nod, not seeming to know anyone he passed.

Must be one of those out-of-towners who'd come to observe the festivities, Sam decided. Maybe hoping to meet women. If so, he should loosen up some. That stiff, rather formal manner was hardly conducive to casual friendly encounters.

Losing interest in the guy, Sam turned to respond to a greeting from a regular diner customer, then to accept a plate from one of the cheerful servers. A glance at the awning let him know that the helpful teenagers Serena had mentioned had already broken in line and snagged meals for the seniors there. He smiled as he watched Marjorie regally pat a boy's arm, wearing the same grandmotherly smile he remembered from his first meeting with her. "Way to go, Marjorie," he murmured.

"Don't encourage her," Serena advised him, overhearing. "She's shameless."

Sam only grinned.

They carried their plates to the lawn chairs they'd brought with them and were soon surrounded by Serena's friends—mostly young married couples, some with small children, and a few singles, Lindsey Gray among them. Serena introduced him to everyone he hadn't met before, her tone very casual, making it quite clear that she and Sam were mere acquaintances. She almost overemphasized that fact. Sam could see that some of her friends were eyeing the two of them curiously, as if wondering what was *really* going on between them.

They'd only shared a couple of kisses, he could have told them. Spectacular kisses, it was true—but that was all there was between them. Maybe he'd thought about kissing her again—okay, he had *definitely* thought about doing it again—but he had enough willpower to resist. At least, he hoped he did.

The gospel quartet had been replaced on the stage by a group of pint-size tap dancers in red, blue and silver-spangled costumes. The daughter of a couple sitting near them was one of the dancers, so everyone turned to watch. Sam found the performance both charming and amusing. As far as he could tell, there wasn't a trace of genuine talent in the entire group of moppets.

"Awful, aren't they?" A lanky-limbed man with brown hair in need of a trim and unusual gray eyes made the comment as he joined them, causing those who overheard him to wince.

"Our daughter's in that group," an indignant mother said, motioning toward her husband.

The newcomer responded with a careless grin. "And they're just as cute as all get-out. But not one of them could dance her way out of a paper bag."

"They're only four and five years old," the mother insisted. "They'll get better with practice."

"That's your kid on the right, isn't it, Claudia?" the man inquired, glancing at the stage.

Claudia preened. "Yes. That's our Stephanie."

"Definitely born with her father's complete lack of rhythm. Sorry, Joe, but you know you've got two left feet. I've seen you dancing—or trying to—over at Gaylord's."

Joe chuckled ruefully. "You're right, Riley, I can't dance worth a lick. I was hoping dance lessons would help Stephanie overcome her hereditary limitations."

"Ain't going to happen," Riley pronounced, settling on the grass not far from Sam's chair. "She's got her mama's pretty face and her old man's endearing clumsiness."

Claudia didn't seem to know whether to be flattered by the offhand compliment or insulted by the repeated aspersions against her daughter's talent.

Riley had already turned his attention elsewhere.

"You must be the guy Lindsey's been telling me about. Sam, right?"

"Yes. And you're Riley, the reporter."

"Bingo." Riley studied him with unselfconscious thoroughness. "How come you wouldn't answer any of Lindsey's questions? Got something you're trying to hide?"

"So, are you *trying* to annoy everyone here?" Serena asked Riley mildly.

He chuckled. "Just trying to spice up the afternoon."

The dance troupe completed their final number—finishing at approximately the same time—and Sam joined the others in enthusiastic applause. So maybe none of them would be joining the Rockettes. They were cute.

"You like kids, Sam?" Lindsey asked, a big slice of watermelon in her hands.

He shrugged. "Sure."

"None of your own?"

He sincerely hoped there weren't any children anywhere crying for their daddy. He felt badly enough to think about any adults who could be sick with worry about him. But the memories were coming back slowly, he reminded himself. Only flashes, of course, and those didn't make much sense at this point, but he was sure it wouldn't be much longer before it all returned.

Only a couple of days remained of the three weeks he'd given himself to fully recover his memory. If it wasn't back by then, he would definitely tell someone. Probably, he amended.

"Sam? I asked if you have any kids," Lindsey prodded.

"Oh, uh, no. No kids." And wouldn't *she* love to know the truth about him? He could already envision the headlines for the story she would write. "Nameless man pulls wool over town's eyes, takes advantage of kindness of locals."

No, he couldn't let Lindsey find out. Not yet, anyway. If he was lucky, not ever.

Because this line of conversation was making him nervous, he decided to put an end to it. Gathering his used paper plate, napkin, plastic cutlery and empty soft drink can, he stacked them in one hand and reached for Serena's trash. "Here, I'll take that for you. I saw some bins on the other side of the stage."

"I can carry my own," she said automatically.

"No need. I'm going anyway."

Probably because it would have looked foolish for her to continue to protest, she conceded. Surely she didn't think his disposing of her trash implied an intimate relationship between them, he thought as he allowed Lindsey to add her used items to the growing pile. It was just a polite gesture, nothing more. There were times when it wouldn't hurt Serena to be a little more like her mother.

He had just dumped the last paper plate in the garbage can when he saw the man he'd noticed before, the one who had seemed so out of place. The guy was standing with his back to Sam, seeming to scan the crowd on the other side of the football field. Even though the sun was beginning to set, the man still wore his designer sunglasses. Apparently, he hadn't made any friends since Sam had first spotted him nearly an hour earlier; he still looked very much alone.

"This guy seems to be seriously socially challenged," he murmured to himself.

Though the stranger was too far away to have heard, he turned at that moment and faced in Sam's direction. Maybe he'd had that universal tingly feeling that someone was watching him. He looked straight at Sam—and froze. Sam could see the guy stiffen. He had a feeling that if he could see the eyes behind the designer sunglasses, they would be wide and startled. Who the hell?

"Excuse me, Sam. I can't get to the trash can." The man Sam knew only as Serena's friend Joe—Claudia's husband and Stephanie's father—stood behind him, his hands filled with used plates and napkins.

"Sorry, Joe. Hey, do you recognize that guy over there?"

Sam turned to point him out—but couldn't find him. Whoever the guy was, he'd disappeared into the crowd. "Never mind. I've lost him."

"Point him out to me if you see him again. I've lived in Edstown all my life. I know most of the folks around here, at least by sight."

Sam had the uncomfortable feeling that Joe wouldn't know this guy.

Who *was* he? And why had he looked at Sam as if he'd been startled to see him there, when Sam would have been willing to bet they'd never met? At least, not since he'd arrived in Edstown. Remembering the way he'd been found—the attack he'd suffered at unknown hands—he wasn't sure this was someone he *wanted* to remember.

Maybe the other man had been surprised to see Sam because he hadn't expected to see him alive.

Or maybe Sam was letting his overactive imagination run away with him. Maybe the guy was just cruising for women and had wondered why Sam was staring at *him*.

Shaking his head in self-disgust, he turned to rejoin the others. A high school concert band was tuning up to perform—at least, he hoped the noises they were making were tune-up sounds and not intended to actually resemble music.

Serena and her friends had no trouble passing the time during the next hour, laughing, cracking jokes, talking so fast their words overlapped. Someone in the group produced a pocket trivia game, and they spent several minutes reading questions from the cards and calling out answers—not playing seriously, just having fun trying to beat each other to the correct answers. Riley turned out to be a near genius with trivia; the others called him a "fount of obscure details."

It frustrated Sam no end that he could remember the answers to so many of those meaningless questions when he couldn't remember anything significant about his own past.

Though the group included Sam in their fun as much as possible, considering that he didn't share their history or their inside jokes, he was content for the most part to watch and listen. He was experiencing another major episode of déjà vu—there was a pleasant familiarity to sitting among a group of friends, listening to their foolishness. He closed his eyes for a moment and could *almost* hear other voices speaking. Men and women, exchanging quips, finishing each other's sentences. People he had known? Imagined? Watched on TV? Who *were* they?

"Sam? Are you okay?"

He opened his eyes to find that Serena had leaned closer to his chair. It was almost dark, and several large stadium lights had been turned on to provide illumination for the festivities. Sam could see the concern in Serena's face. "I'm fine," he assured her. "Just enjoying the evening."

"You were frowning as though you were straining to remember something vitally important."

He didn't quite know how to respond to that except to say, "Was I?"

He should have remembered that it annoyed Serena when he responded to her comments with cryptic questions. She sighed. "Do you want anything to eat? They're selling ice cream bars and popcorn for those who like to snack during the fireworks show."

Shaking his head, he declined politely. "I ate too much earlier. The fireworks should be starting soon, shouldn't they?"

"Another ten or fifteen minutes, I think. They'll turn the stadium lights off just before the fireworks start."

Serena's estimate had been accurate. It was just over ten minutes later when the big lights flashed a couple of times, then went out, leaving the stadium darkened except for a few security lights at either end. Taped patriotic music swelled through somewhat scratchy speakers, and a ripple of anticipation went through the crowd. The scent of insect repellant was heavy around them; folks had been splashing and spraying since sunset, even though Sam hadn't been bothered by the bloodthirsty critters. He could still smell watermelon and smoldering charcoals, along with the slightest hint of plain old sweat. The air smelled like the Fourth of July, he thought, then wondered how he knew that.

The fireworks show began with a noisy eruption of light and color. The crowd obligingly oohed and aahed. Sam remembered fireworks. He enjoyed them. But even more than the intricately designed explosions, he enjoyed watching Serena's face during the show. The fireworks reflected in her widened eyes and illuminated her fair skin. When he'd first seen her, he'd thought her very pretty. As he'd gotten to know her better, he'd realized that she was quite beautiful.

It was hard to look away from her. He didn't want to be too obvious about it. Her friends were curious enough. Besides, he was aware that she was surreptitiously watching him in return.

The fireworks display ended with a suitably awe-inspiring finale and the national anthem. Brought to their feet, the crowd applauded, then began to gather their belongings and move toward the exits. Sam was amazed by how quickly the stadium emptied. Having bade good evening to her friends, Marjorie rejoined Serena and Sam, looking as if she'd enjoyed herself immensely. "Did you kids have fun?"

"I did," Sam assured her. "And you?"

"Oh, I had a wonderful time. Serena, did you know Virginia's granddaughter, Melinda, is already filing for a divorce? Rumor has it that her new husband never really broke things off with his old girlfriend, if you know what I mean."

Serena motioned toward the nearest exit gate. "You can tell me all the latest gossip on the way home, if you want."

They were walking through the shadowy, rapidly emptying parking lot when Sam's attention was captured by a familiar young voice. "I'm sorry," the kid was saying. "I didn't mean to—it was an accident."

"You little brat, you spilled grape soda all over my lawn chair. That purple stuff will never come off the fabric. I knew I should've made you sit on the ground, but your mama said you had to have a chair like the rest of us. Now you've ruined it.''

"It was an accident, Delbert,'' the boy insisted, looking apprehensive, Sam thought. "Someone bumped the back of the chair, and the drink spilled.''

Sam immediately identified the sandy-haired kid as Zach, the boy he'd met outside the candy store. He had turned just in time to see a big-bellied man with thinning hair pulled into a scraggly ponytail reach out to give the boy a shove that nearly knocked him off his feet.

"How many times have I told you to be careful with my stuff?'' the guy roared. "You're going to pay for this chair, you hear me? Even if I gotta take it outta your hide.''

A woman with bleached blond hair, too-tight clothes and a whiny voice stood nearby, wringing her hands. "He said he didn't mean to, Delbert.''

"Shut up. It ain't your chair he messed up. I told you he didn't need one, but I let you talk me into it, and now look what happened.''

"But he—''

The big man threw the folded, green-fabric-covered lawn chair at her. She barely caught it before it hit her. "Put that in the back of the truck, then get inside,'' he ordered. "I'll take care of your kid, since you ain't going to.''

"Can't we just go home?'' Zach asked miserably, noticing Sam watching them. "Everybody's looking at us. I'll try to clean the chair when we get home.''

"I don't give a damn who's looking at us,'' Delbert snarled, turning on the boy, his hand poised for a back-handed slap. "You ain't running things around here, you little—"

Sam caught the guy's swinging hand in midair. "You might want to reconsider that move," he advised coldly, too furious to care that he was hardly a physical match for this man who had a couple of inches of height and maybe fifty pounds of weight advantage.

Sam would be damned if he was going to stand by and watch this jerk hit a defenseless little kid, even if interfering landed him back in the hospital.

Chapter Ten

Delbert had never heard Sam approach, obviously. He shook off Sam's hand. "Who the hell are you?" he asked. Though alcoholic beverages had been prohibited at the festivities, this guy's breath and behavior indicated he'd found a way to smuggle some in.

"The name's Sam. And I think you'd better cool off before you do something you'll regret."

"You're going to regret you ever came here tonight if you don't butt out of my business." Delbert turned to give Zach another shove that nearly knocked the boy down. "Get in the damned truck."

Watching the child stumble as he tried desperately to catch his balance made Sam grind his teeth. He shot a hard look at the bleached blonde. "What kind of mother stands by and lets a big jerk like that hit her kid?"

She flushed and gave Delbert a frightened look.

"We better just go, okay? We don't want any trouble."

"Yeah. We'll finish this when we get home." The menace in Delbert's voice made both the woman and the boy quail.

Sam stepped between Delbert and the battered truck. "You lay a hand on that boy tonight, or any other time, and I'll make sure you never get close enough to touch him again."

He knew he was being reckless, interfering in a domestic situation that was technically none of his business, but he couldn't stand the thought that no one was watching out for this boy's welfare. Somebody had to put Zach first— and it obviously wasn't going to be his mother.

Delbert took another step toward Sam, until his belly was only inches from Sam's tightly cinched belt. "I don't know who you are," he said, his voice low. "But you're making an enemy you don't want."

"And so are you," Sam answered smoothly.

"What's going on here?" Dan Meadows appeared out of the shadows, his hands on his hips, his voice stern. Serena and Marjorie stood close behind him; Sam assumed they had summoned him.

The look Delbert gave Dan indicated there were plenty of hard feelings between the two. "This a friend of yours, *Chief?*" He emphasized the title with a sneer.

"I know him. What's the problem?"

"You need to teach your pal not to interfere with people he doesn't know. We were just minding our own business when he assaulted us."

Since Dan's gaze went directly to the miserable looking Zach, Sam figured the chief guessed what had caused the confrontation. "Oh, I doubt Sam assaulted you. More likely he just wanted to introduce himself. He's new in town, aren't you, Sam?"

Sam nodded.

Delbert's scowl intensified as he realized he would get no sympathy from Dan. He pointed a finger at Sam. "You stay away from me and mine," he muttered.

"It's a small town," Sam answered evenly. "I'm sure I'll see you around."

Delbert shot another angry look at Dan, then shouldered past Sam. "Rita, Zach—get in the truck."

"I'll be in your neighborhood quite a bit during the next couple of weeks," Dan said as Sam moved reluctantly out of the way. "I'll probably stop by a few times to same hello to my buddy Zach."

In other words, he would be watching for bruises or any signs of abuse. Sam was far from satisfied with the veiled warning. "That's all you're going to do?" he asked Dan as Delbert's truck spat gravel on its departure from the parking lot.

"That's all I *can* do," Dan reminded him tersely. "You didn't actually see him hit the boy, did you?"

"He shoved him. Twice. Nearly knocked him off his feet both times. And he had his hand raised to hit him when I stepped in."

Dan glanced at Serena and Marjorie. "Did either of you see Delbert shove the kid?"

Serena shook her head. "I was unlocking my car. I didn't realize Sam wasn't behind me until I heard Delbert's voice raised. That's when I saw what was going on and started looking for you."

"I didn't see it, either," Marjorie admitted. And

then her face brightened. "But I'll say I did if it will help Zach."

Dan winced. "Uh, no. We can't do that." He turned to Sam again. "Look, I know you're concerned about the boy. I am, too. I'll talk to Rita again—though God knows she's so scared of Delbert, she won't do much to interfere with him."

"Then why does she keep the bastard around? They're not married, right?"

"No. But cases like this are so damned frustrating because of that very thing—the women are more scared of being alone, for some reason, than they are of being knocked around. Or maybe they're afraid to try to get out of the relationship for fear of reprisal. That's the most dangerous time in an abusive relationship—when the victim tries to break away."

"But—"

Dan held up a hand. "I'll contact the Department of Human Services, ask them to look into the home conditions there again, okay? They've gotten involved before, but they haven't done much. They're overworked and understaffed, and their efforts have to be primarily focused on the most critical cases, but they'll send someone to talk to Delbert and Rita and Zach. And I'll be very visible to all three of them for the next few weeks. For now, that's all I can do. Or you, either," he added warningly. "Unless you've got some desire to end up in the hospital again."

Sam scowled. "In other words, until the kid has some broken bones or a concussion or a couple dozen stitches, Delbert's off the hook."

"I'm going to do my best to keep it from getting to that point. But in the meantime, you stay out of it, you hear? You're only going to make the whole situation worse if you set Delbert off again.''

There was nothing left for Sam to say. He knew Dan was doing what he could, but it was damned frustrating to know something was going on and not be able to put an end to it.

Serena and Sam lingered in the garage after Marjorie went inside. The ride home had been a bit tense, Marjorie filling in the silence between Serena and Sam with a recap of the evening's juiciest gossip. Neither of her listeners had made much comment.

After Marjorie excused herself with a claim of fatigue that was obviously a ruse to leave them alone, Serena turned to Sam. "I have to ask—do you *want* to get beaten up again?"

"Hardly."

"Delbert Farley is the meanest, most obnoxious and aggressive man in this town. He's been in jail several times. Two of my clients are pursuing legal damages against him because of his viciousness and destructiveness and—"

"He hits little kids," Sam cut in, folding his arms across his chest. "At least one little kid. Zach. The boy's terrified of him, and obviously for good reason."

"I'm sure you meant well, but don't you understand that interfering in domestic cases is dangerous? You could have been badly hurt. What if he'd hit you in the ribs? Or what if you'd fallen and hit your head? You might have made an incredibly fast recovery last time, but if you'd reinjured those—"

"What would you have had me do, Serena?" he

interrupted to ask. "Stand there and watch him back-hand that boy?"

"No, of course not. You could have done what Mother and I did—found Dan and let him handle the situation."

"By the time I'd done that, Farley would have already hit the boy and left."

"It's Dan's job to deal with that sort of thing."

"It's *everyone's* job," Sam snapped. "When the parents won't protect a child, someone else has to step in. When they don't, the kid's on his own—completely helpless, alone, trusting no one because he doesn't know who he *can* trust."

Serena was taken aback by the bitterness in Sam's voice. The underlying hints of pain. Was he describing his own childhood? Was that why he was so reluctant to talk about his past? Was that why he had no family to turn to now? "Sam?"

His jaw tightened. "It just made me mad to see that jerk pushing Zach around."

It abruptly occurred to her that she was criticizing him for doing something that had been very courageous and well-intentioned. Though the bruises from his injuries still hadn't completely faded and the scar from his stitches was still livid against his forehead, he had risked personal injury to protect a small boy he didn't even know. Would she really have admired him more if he had looked the other way?

"I'm sorry," she said, holding up both hands in an apologetic gesture. "Of course you did the right thing. I was just worried that Delbert would hurt you, too."

He seemed to relax a little at that. Uncrossing his arms, he reached out to touch her face. "You were worried about me?"

When she'd turned to see Sam in a confrontation with Delbert Farley, her heart had almost stopped. Everyone knew Delbert was someone to be avoided, especially when he was in a temper. He was mean and unpredictable, quick with his fists and unconcerned with consequences. He could have done serious damage to Sam before Serena had arrived with Dan. She'd worried the whole time.

"I really am capable of taking care of myself, you know," Sam said.

"I don't doubt that you are," she replied, though she still remembered the way he'd looked when she'd found him. "But you aren't fully recovered yet, no matter how much you pretend you're no longer in any pain."

He was standing very close to her, the back of his hand resting against her cheek. Finding herself suddenly lost in his eyes, she almost forgot what she'd been fussing about. Funny how she was beginning to think the garage was a romantic place. She'd been spending way too much time in here with Sam.

He seemed to somehow know what she was thinking. He glanced around the garage, then looked at her with a slightly rueful smile. "We really have to stop meeting like this."

The bad cliché broke the spell she'd almost fallen into. She returned the smile with a faint one of her own. "You're right."

"Except for the episode with Farley, I enjoyed your Independence Day celebration. Thanks for including me with your friends."

"I'm glad you had a good time. And there's no such thing as too many friends."

"Right. So…" He ran his knuckles lightly down the line of her jaw. "Good night, friend."

She maintained her smile with an effort. "Good night, Sam."

His gaze was on her mouth when his hand fell to his side. Neither of them made the first move away. And, suddenly, neither of them was smiling.

"Serena?" His voice was husky.

Hers was a whisper. "Yes?"

"You'd better go in. Now."

"I know." But still she didn't move.

Sam put his hands on her shoulders and turned her toward the exit. "Go."

She couldn't resist looking over her shoulder again. Their eyes met—and Sam sighed. "Well," he murmured, "I tried."

A moment later, she was in his arms, her lips smothered beneath his. The fireworks they'd viewed at the Independence Day celebration were nothing in comparison to the ones that exploded in Serena's mind when Sam pulled her closer to his lean, hard body and swept her mouth with his tongue.

Serena had tried repeatedly to convince herself that her sister had inherited all the reckless genes in the family. Yet every time Sam kissed her, she responded with an enthusiasm that belied that long-held assumption.

She didn't respond this way to other men. She'd always prided herself on being practical and rational, even in matters of romance. She didn't let herself be led by instinct or controlled by hormones. Yet, somehow, here she was, being kissed senseless in her garage by a man who appealed directly to both her instincts and her hormones. A man her rational mind kept trying to warn her away from.

Sam's hands were cupped around her bottom, pressing her against his arousal. Was she reminding herself that this was rash and imprudent behavior? No. She was reveling in it.

Even when she found herself pressed against the paneled wall, his leg between hers, his mouth devouring hers, did she push him away and inform him that she had no interest in pursuing this further? No. She did everything she could to pull him closer.

This time it was Sam who broke the kiss off with a gasp and a groan. If he hadn't, Serena couldn't have said how far the embrace might have gone. He didn't immediately release her, but stood with his forehead against hers, his breathing uneven as he took a moment to regain his equilibrium. Serena thought it might take quite a while for her to recover her own.

"There's something about you," he said after a long moment, "that makes me forget every promise I make to myself. Something that completely destroys my willpower."

"Trust me," she murmured after moistening her tender lips, "I know the feeling."

"There's something I need to talk to you about," he said, lifting his head. "Soon. But not here," he added, glancing around the garage. "Not tonight. It's late, and you're probably tired."

This was definitely not the time to talk about anything important. She could barely speak, much less think clearly enough to concentrate on a conversation. Still, she was curious. "What do you want to talk about?"

He seemed about to answer—but then he stopped and shook his head. "Later."

She studied his face. That lost look was in his eyes again, the one that sneaked behind the few defenses she had left against him. She found it hard to believe he could deliberately assume that expression, for whatever reason. There was a sadness in Sam she didn't understand and didn't know how to alleviate.

She remembered something LuWanda, one of his hospital nurses, had said about him. "Have you seen the look in his eyes? Something tragic happened to him—maybe the death of someone he loved deeply or something awful like that. He's running from a broken heart or tragic memories. I'd bet my next week's salary on it."

Maybe it was that alleged tragedy Sam wanted to talk to her about. But not tonight.

Realizing she was still standing in his arms, their bodies still intimately pressed together, she eased away from him. "We'll talk tomorrow," she said— and in the meantime, she would do everything she could to reinforce those very precarious defenses.

Sam pushed his hands in his pockets. This time, he made no move to detain her when she turned and moved toward the door.

The big gossip at the diner the next day was that someone had broken into the candy store, trashed the place and stolen an unspecified amount of money from the cash register. It happened sometime between midnight and three o'clock, according to the reports Sam heard. There couldn't have been much money in the store, but it had certainly been easy enough to break into, with its end-of-the-street location, big windows and lack of a security system.

"What is the world coming to?" Justine fussed to Sam during a lull in luncheon business. "Seems like every time I turn around, I'm hearing about another crime in this town. Home break-ins, your mugging and now this. I can tell you, folks are starting to wonder what Dan Meadows is doing to earn his salary. I heard the mayor had quite a long talk with him this morning."

Sam hated hearing his tale in the list of unsolved crimes being held against the affable police chief. Serena was definitely not the only one in this town to whom he owed an apology and the truth. "I'm sure Chief Meadows will solve these cases soon. He seems to take his responsibilities very seriously."

"Oh, I like Dan—just about everyone does," Justine assured him. "We just want to keep him on his toes."

Sam, for one, was glad *he* didn't have Dan's very publicly scrutinized job.

Dan walked into the diner just as Marjorie hung the Closed sign in the window that afternoon. "Hey, Dan," Sam greeted him, knowing this particular customer was welcome at any time. "Can I get you some iced tea or a cup of coffee?"

"Tea sounds good. It's hot as blue blazes out there." Dan glanced at Marjorie. "You mind if Sam and I sit and talk for a few minutes? I won't keep him long."

"Go right ahead," Marjorie replied with a smile. "Sam's pretty much finished for the day, anyway. How about a piece of pie to go with that tea? We've got a couple slices of lemon icebox left."

"No, thanks." Dan made a rueful face as he patted his stomach. "My pants seem to be shrinking a bit lately. Guess I'd better start cutting back on the sweets before I end up with a belly like my dad's."

"Your father's not fat—he's just robust," Marjorie assured him kindly.

Dan laughed. "Well, I'd like to be just a little less robust than Dad. Sam," he added as Sam carried two glasses of tea toward him, "let's take that booth in the back, shall we?"

It was obvious that Dan wanted to talk in private. Sam suspected the chief wasn't going to invite him fishing this time. As always, he wondered exactly what Dan had discovered since the last time they'd talked. Did Dan know more about him than Sam knew himself?

"What is it, Chief?" he asked when they were seated in the relatively isolated booth, out of hearing of the other diner employees who were preparing to leave for the day.

Dan took a sip of the tea, then set the glass on the table. "You called me Dan when we went fishing."

"You weren't on duty then. I get the feeling you are now."

Dan grimaced. "I'm afraid so. I guess you heard about the candy store."

Sam lifted an eyebrow. This was a topic he hadn't expected. "Yeah, sure. Everyone was talking about it this morning. Why?"

"I got an anonymous tip that you were seen loitering on Main Street at about two this morning. That's about the time we figure the candy store was hit."

Scowling, Sam shook his head. "Your informant was mistaken. I was in bed at two. I didn't leave the guest house until Marjorie drove me to work this morning.''

"I don't suppose you have anyone who can verify that.''

"I was in bed *alone*,'' Sam said flatly. "C'mon, Dan, what's this all about? You know I didn't knock over the candy store.''

Dan pushed a hand through his brown hair, leaving it standing in disheveled spikes. "Hell, Sam, I didn't say I believed it. But when I get a call like that, I have to follow up on it.''

"The caller specified me by name?''

"Actually, he called you 'that stranger who's been mooching off the Schaffer women.''''

This time it was Sam's turn to wince. A curse escaped him before he could bite it back.

Dan's shrug was faintly apologetic. "You asked.''

"Who would—'' For some reason, Sam thought of the eccentric-acting stranger he'd spotted twice during the Independence Day celebration. And then he thought of the way that celebration had ended. "Oh, hell.''

Dan seemed to follow his line of thinking. "Yeah. It was probably Delbert Farley—or one of his pals. But whoever it was called from a pay phone and refused to give a name.''

"So, do you think Farley broke into the candy store and blamed me for it?''

"I dropped by their place this morning. He and Rita both swear they never left their trailer last night. A neighbor confirmed that he saw Delbert's truck in the driveway when he got home from a seven-to-three shift at the plant. If it was Delbert who called me, he might well have just heard about the break-in and decided to cause trouble for you in return for you causing trouble for him at the stadium.''

"So what are you going to do now? Arrest me?''

"Not on the basis of one anonymous phone call. Give me a little credit, will you, Sam?''

And now Sam was feeling guilty again. Dan was showing him a trust that Sam wasn't giving in return. Dan had been nothing but honest with Sam, while Sam had lied to Dan from the start. "Uh, Dan—''

A shrill ring interrupted him. Dan answered his wireless phone, said a few words, then pushed his empty tea glass away. "I've got to go. I just thought I should give you a heads-up that you've made yourself an enemy around here.''

Funny. Sam thought of himself as a decent enough guy, despite his lack of memory about his past. Yet someone had beaten him to a pulp three weeks ago, and now someone else was trying to have him arrested. Heck of a track record.

"I'll see you around, Sam,'' Dan said over his shoulder as he moved toward the door.

"Yeah. See you, Dan.'' Thoughtfully, Sam watched the chief leave.

He'd been on the verge of telling Dan everything, he realized. Which he needed to do—but maybe he should tell Serena first.

Sam told Marjorie to go home without him. He had some things to do in town, he told her. He would walk home.

His first stop after leaving the diner was the library. Nodding to the friendly librarian, he didn't pause to chat, but headed straight for the computers. He spent the next couple of hours searching the Internet, look-

ing for any information about a missing person who
even roughly matched his description. Keeping Serena's guesses in mind, he concentrated on Texas and
then expanded his search, but he still came up blank.
If anyone was looking for him, he found no evidence
of it.

The research he did on amnesia proved little more
helpful than his search for his identity. He learned
nothing new, only the same facts he'd read before.
True amnesia was very rare, little understood and in-
consistently treated. The prognosis seemed to be different with each case, some patients recovering almost
miraculously, some partially—and some never regaining their memories.

In every article, the victims were considered medical oddities. Intriguing case studies.

Weird, he elaborated glumly. The word wasn't used
in any of the articles, but it might as well have been,
as far as he was concerned. Once word got out about
his condition, he would be "that weird guy who
doesn't know his name"—in addition to "that
stranger who's been mooching off the Schaffer
women," as the anonymous caller had identified him
to Dan.

He wasn't ready to go back to the guest house when
he left the library. He spent the rest of the afternoon
walking the streets of downtown, his hands in his
pockets, his eyes shaded by the cap Dan had given
him for their fishing trip. As he walked, he futilely
probed his mind for memories. He was aware of people passing, even absently returned a few greetings,
but he knew he would never be able to list those he'd
passed. He couldn't concentrate on anything but the

mess he'd gotten himself into with his stubbornness and his pride.

Serena was never going to trust him again, he decided glumly. And why should she? All he had done was lie to her.

Maybe he should just leave town. He could find a job somewhere else while he recovered his memory, send money to the hospital when he could. At least that way he wouldn't risk hurting anyone here with further deceptions. And he wouldn't risk being thrown in jail because someone here had it in for him, he added with grim humor as his gaze skimmed the candy store at the end of the street. Yellow police tape decorated the front of the store, and the broken window had been hastily covered with plywood.

Had to be the work of punk kids, he thought with a disgusted shake of his head. Who else would break into a candy store for what little cash had been left overnight? Surely even Farley hadn't been stupid enough to pull this stunt just to spite Sam.

Still lost in thought, he turned to head in the other direction, telling himself he might as well face the music eventually. He had to tell Serena the truth before anything further happened between them. He wasn't looking forward to it, but if he was going to stay here, it had to be done. It was either that or sneak out during the night—and she deserved better than that. So did Marjorie.

He glanced around. There weren't many people on the sidewalks this late in the afternoon, but there was one he wasn't at all pleased to see. Wearing a blue work shirt that indicated he'd just gotten off work at the muffler shop, Delbert Farley stood on the other side of Main Street, glaring. Sam remembered the anonymous call to Dan, and his temper flared. If Farley had pulled that stupid stunt, he should know it hadn't worked—and that he'd better not try it again.

He had just stepped into the street to cross to the other side when the sudden roar of a car's engine pulled his attention away from Farley. The street had been deserted of traffic when he'd stepped onto it—or so he'd thought—but now a large, dark SUV was bearing down on him. Fast.

Sam jumped over the yellow line in the center of the street, out of the vehicle's lane. The SUV swerved, keeping him directly in its path.

Though he wasn't sure he could reach it in time, Sam made a desperate dive for the sidewalk.

Chapter Eleven

Serena knew about the anonymous call to Dan. Word traveled fast in Edstown, particularly in the small legal community. Someone told someone who told someone who told Serena—and she got the distinct impression that whoever had made the accusatory call had wanted the news to get out. Someone wanted to cast suspicion on Sam—and she had a pretty good idea who it could be.

He wasn't there when she got home Thursday evening, and neither was her mother. A note on the refrigerator door let her know that her mother had gone to a movie with a couple of her friends. There was no mention of Sam's whereabouts.

Maybe Sam was with Dan, Serena speculated as she let Walter into the backyard for some fresh air and exercise. Though she'd heard Dan wasn't taking the anonymous tip very seriously, she supposed he had to follow up on it. Maybe he'd taken Sam in for questioning. Or maybe they'd gone fishing again.

The phone rang and she snatched it up, closing the kitchen door with the hope that Sam's fence repairs would keep Walter from wandering this time. "Hello?"

"Oh, Serena. Hi. You sound as if you're expecting a call." Kara's tone was a bit stiff—probably because she knew Serena still didn't approve of Kara's decision to leave Edstown with her boyfriend.

"No," Serena said, equally awkward. "I wasn't really expecting a call. I just happened to be standing by the phone. I'm sure you called to talk to Mother, but she isn't home right now."

"Oh. Well—how are you?"

"I'm fine, thank you. And you?"

"Just fine. Thanks for asking."

This was ridiculous. As close as they had once been, they were speaking like mere passing acquaintances. Remembering Sam's criticisms, Serena was determined to prove she wasn't being petty or selfish just because she thought Kara had made an imprudent decision. "How's Pierce?"

"He's great." Kara's voice was suddenly more animated. "He's getting a lot of attention with his singing. One of the club regulars knows a guy who's a good friend of a very reputable music agent. The club customer is going to bring in his friend to hear Pierce sing and maybe the friend will convince the agent to consider Pierce as a client."

Couldn't Kara hear how improbable that all sounded? Pierce's odds of being discovered by the friend of a friend of an agent were probably less than his chances of being kidnapped by Martians—but she was determined to be pleasant. "That's wonderful. I'm sure I'll be hearing him on the radio any day now."

"You think no such thing," Kara replied a bit peevishly. "But you'll see. Pierce *will* make it. It only takes one lucky break."

"Then I hope that break comes soon. For both your sakes."

"Thanks—but in the meantime, we're very happy together. And now," she added before Serena had to come up with yet another optimistic platitude, "tell me more about this guy living in the guest house. I can tell Mom's fond of him, but she hasn't told me much about him."

"That's because we don't know very much about him," Serena answered, her muscles tensing again. "He rarely talks about himself."

"I have to admit I was surprised to hear that you'd allowed her to let a homeless drifter move into the guest house. That sounds like such an illogical decision on your part."

It was a deliberate goad, but Serena refused to fall for it. She was more offended by Kara's description of Sam than she was by the implied criticism of her customary caution. "Sam's a nice guy. A hard worker who's trying to pay off the debts he has incurred here through no fault of his own. He's courteous and quiet and considerate, going out of his way to help out around the place. All the customers at the diner like him—even Dan likes him, and you know how cautious *he* is about people."

"Goodness." There was a faint hint of amusement in Kara's voice now. "It sounds as if you rather like him yourself."

"I like him well enough." Serena found it difficult

to maintain an offhand tone when her mind was suddenly filled with memories of kisses that still curled her toes.

"Mom said he's young and good-looking. True?"

"He just turned thirty-one."

"And good-looking?"

He was gorgeous, of course, but Serena had no intention of saying so at the moment. Not when it was obvious that Kara was just looking for a reason to pick on her. "He's attractive, I suppose."

"Mom said he looks like a male model or something—blond hair, blue eyes, killer smile. Was she exaggerating?"

"Why don't you come see for yourself?" Serena challenged. "Mother would love a visit from you— and, by the way, there are a few things at the paper that need your attention."

A heavy sigh came through the phone line. "I promised Mom I'll come home for a visit as soon as I can. As for the paper, I'm sorry, but I'm no longer responsible. I quit. I regret that you ended up in a position you didn't want, but I told you I thought you should sell the paper. There are several media groups interested in buying small-town newspapers for the local advertising revenue."

"You know how Mother feels about that."

"I know she doesn't want to sell, but she'll get over it. She wouldn't want you to be miserable, even to keep the paper in the family."

"What she wants is for you to come home and stop wasting your education and experience schlepping drinks in some bar."

"No. That's what *you* want me to do," Kara countered flatly. "Mother just wants me to be happy. And I am."

"I just hope that doesn't suddenly change."

"It won't. Pierce and I were meant to be together. I'm just sorry you don't have anyone who makes you as happy as we are."

Serena decided it would be better to bite her tongue than to try to come up with a response to that.

After a moment, Kara sighed again. "Never mind. Perhaps you'll never understand how it feels to love someone so much you're willing to sacrifice everything. I guess you just aren't programmed that way."

Serena rather resented being made to sound like a computer. She was quite capable of falling in love— she had simply planned to do so at her own pace, and much more sensibly than Kara had done. Infatuation was one thing—but sacrifice everything for a man? That wasn't something she had ever intended to do.

Of course, she hadn't ever expected to fall head over heels for a mysterious drifter, either—but it was getting harder with each passing hour to convince herself she hadn't done just that. How could she continue to criticize Kara when she was getting entirely too involved with a man who could very easily turn her world topsy-turvy?

"Tell Mom I called and that I'll talk to her later, okay? And, Serena—I really am sorry about the trouble I've caused you. But that's my only regret about the choices I've made. The real regrets would have come if I'd chosen *not* to take a chance on love."

"Just…take care of yourself, Kara."

Serena had hardly hung up the phone when someone tapped on the kitchen door. *Sam,* she thought, her pulse suddenly accelerating.

She gasped when she opened the door and saw him. "What happened to you *now?*"

Sam had expected Serena to react dramatically to his freshly battered appearance. There was a raw scrape on his chin and a new bruise on his jaw. His right knee, abraded and bloody, was visible through a rip in his jeans. He'd considered cleaning up before letting her see him, but he'd been concerned that someone else would call her before he could tell her about the latest incident that had happened to him. He wanted to be the one to break it to her before she got the gossip-enhanced version. "I had a little accident, but I'm fine, okay?"

"You don't look fine." She took his arm and pulled him inside. "What happened? Did you fall?"

"Let's just say I had a close encounter with the sidewalk on Main Street. Is your mother here?"

"No, she's out with friends for the evening. Did you walk all the way here? Like this?" She almost pushed him into a chair at the table.

Stretching his throbbing right leg in front of him, he shook his head. "Red Tucker was coming out of the insurance office next to the candy store when the, er, accident happened. He gave me a lift here."

"He should have taken you straight to the hospital. I'll get my car keys and we'll—"

"No." He stopped her by catching her wrist. "No hospitals."

"But Dr. Frank should—"

"No doctors, either. I've only got a few bruises, Serena. Nothing life-threatening, I assure you."

She didn't look satisfied, but she stopped tugging at her wrist. Apparently, his tone had convinced her that he wasn't going to change his mind. "At least let me clean the wounds and apply some ointment."

He nodded. "Actually, I was going to ask to borrow some first aid supplies."

"I'll get the first aid kid. Sit tight."

"I'm not going anywhere." He suppressed a wince as he shifted his right leg to a slightly more comfortable position.

She wasn't gone long. When she returned, she carried a first aid kit in one hand and a pair of navy gym shorts in the other. "Take off your jeans."

He couldn't help grinning in response to her brusque tone. Before he could utter the response that immediately sprang to his mind, she leveled a finger at him. "Don't even think about saying that."

He immediately adopted an innocent expression. "What?"

"Whatever you were going to say." She tossed the shorts on the table. "These were my father's. You can wear them while I work on your knee."

He stood, balancing carefully on his good leg, toed off his shoes and reached for the snap of his torn jeans. Serena turned around, busying herself making a pitcher of iced tea. "You don't need any help, do you?" she asked without turning to look at him.

"If I say yes, will you help?" he asked, peeling shredded denim carefully away from his injured knee.

"Only if you make me believe you really need it."

He chuckled. A moment later, he was decently covered in his scuffed T-shirt, borrowed gym shorts and white tube socks. He lowered himself into the chair again, studying his knee. Not so bad, he decided. Compared to the way he'd looked before, this was just a scratch.

Judging from Serena's scowl, she didn't agree with his assessment. "You must have really hit the pavement hard," she fretted, kneeling beside his chair with a bottle of hydrogen peroxide. "I'll have to clean this before I can put anything on it."

He sipped the iced tea she'd handed him, then said, "I'm perfectly capable of taking care of this myself, you know."

"I just want to make sure it doesn't get infected." She carefully poured the hydrogen peroxide over the oozing wound, watching as it bubbled away impurities. When she was satisfied that his knee was clean enough, she carefully spread a thin layer of medicated cream over the scrape, her fingers no heavier than butterfly wings against his skin. Her head was bent industriously over the task, and it was all Sam could do to prevent himself from running his fingers through her glossy hair.

There should be nothing in the least erotic about the way she touched him—she was obviously making an effort to keep her actions efficient and impersonal—but her touch aroused him anyway.

Bad timing, dude, he reminded himself, knowing he still had to tell her what had happened. He wasn't looking forward to it—he had a feeling she wasn't going to take it well—but she would hear it from him or someone else. He half expected the phone to ring any minute with someone wanting to gossip about the near tragedy on Main Street.

She covered his knee with a gauze pad and secured it with strips of adhesive. "I guess that will have to do," she said, studying the bandage with a frown. "It's going to be sore tomorrow."

"That's okay. I'm getting used to it."

She laid her fingers against his cheek, turning his head to give her a better view of his chin. "This one's not so bad," she murmured, reaching for her supplies again. "Probably won't even need a bandage."

"Good. I'm not wearing a bandage on my chin."

Her eyes lifted for a moment to meet his. "Opinionated, today, aren't you?" She sounded a bit more relaxed now that she'd determined for herself that he wasn't seriously hurt, which was good, considering what he still had to tell her.

Her face was very close to his as she tended to his chin. Moving forward only a couple of inches would bring their mouths together. His hands rested safely on his thighs, but he had only to lift them to have Serena in his arms. His fingers twitched with an urge to do just that; he closed them into loose fists to keep them where they were.

Satisfied that his chin was clean and treated, she studied the bruise on his cheek. "Honestly, Sam, you're starting to resemble a patchwork quilt. You've got bruises in a half dozen different colors."

He gave a rueful shrug. "I seem to be accident prone lately." Had he always been, or was this new for him?

"How in the world did you fall this hard?" she asked as she slid the washcloth over his cheek. "Was there a broken place in the sidewalk?"

Regretfully, he drew his gaze away from the intriguingly gaping scoop neck of her T-shirt. "You aren't going to like this."

The washcloth stilled against his face. She frowned into his eyes. "What do you mean?"

"Some moron in an SUV almost ran me down in

the middle of Main Street. I had to dive out of the way—and I hit the sidewalk harder than I'd intended.''

''Someone almost hit you?'' Her eyes had gone very wide, her cheeks draining of color. ''How? Did the driver run a red light or something? He didn't see you? You didn't see him?''

''I don't know. I'd have sworn there was no vehicle approaching when I started across the street, and then suddenly there was a big, dark SUV bearing right down on me.''

''How close was it?''

He grimaced, almost feeling the whoosh of hot air against his skin again. ''Too damned close.''

Her hand fell to his shoulder, resting there in an almost protective gesture. ''Who was driving? I hope you let the idiot have it for his carelessness.''

''He, uh, didn't stop.''

That brought the color back into her face in a wave of temper. ''He didn't *stop?* You mean, he nearly hit you and then just drove on?''

''Yeah, that pretty much describes it.''

''Is there any chance he didn't see you?''

Remembering his very narrow escape, Sam shook his head. ''He saw me.''

''What kind of jerk would pull a stunt like that? You said Red Tucker saw the entire incident?''

''Yes. Apparently, he stepped out of the insurance company at approximately the same time I noticed the vehicle myself.''

''Red's the best mechanic in the area. He knows what everyone drives, whether he works on their cars or not. Did he recognize the SUV?''

''He said he'd never seen it before. That seemed to disturb him.''

"Did you contact Dan? He should know there's a reckless fool endangering lives around here."

"I haven't talked to him. I'm sure he'll hear about it, though," he added in resignation.

"Good."

"Serena—there's one other thing you need to know," he said reluctantly.

She tilted her head, as if she was preparing herself for another unpleasant shock. "What now?"

"It's about Red Tucker and what he's probably telling everyone. He, uh, has this wild idea that the driver deliberately tried to hit me."

"He *what?*"

Sam suppressed a wince when her hand tightened so forcefully on his shoulder that her short nails dug through his shirt. It felt as though he might have a couple more bruises in the morning—a bit more decoration for the patchwork, he thought wryly, remembering the imagery she'd used.

Shaking his head, he tried to speak reassuringly. "It's a crazy idea, of course. I tried to convince Red that he had to be mistaken, but he wouldn't listen. He said the SUV was parked until I stepped into the road, at which time the driver gunned the motor and headed straight for me. When I tried to move out of the way, the SUV seemed to follow."

"Oh, my God." Her face had gone white again.

On impulse, he reached up to catch her forearms and pull her onto his lap. Caught off guard, she didn't have time to resist, but she made an effort to avoid landing on his injured knee. "Serena, listen to me. Red's obviously a guy with a colorful imagination and a flair for the dramatic. He interpreted what he saw in a way that makes for a good story, that's all."

"Red's dramatic, but he doesn't just make details up out of thin air," she argued. "If he said the driver headed straight for you, then you should take him seriously. You could have been killed."

He could feel her shaking and knew she was imagining the grim scenarios that had played through his mind during the brief drive here. To distract her, he finally allowed himself to run his fingers through her soft hair. Or at least he told himself it was to distract her and not because he'd been wanting to do this since she'd knelt beside his chair. "I'm starting to sort of like it when you worry about me," he murmured. "Even if you do get kind of naggy."

"Naggy?" Her scowl deepened. "I am not naggy. I just—"

Whatever excuse she might have offered, it was lost when his mouth covered hers.

Serena dove into the kiss, thinking of how easily Sam could have been killed that afternoon. It was bad enough remembering how badly he'd been hurt before, but the thought of losing him that way now, after they'd shared kisses that affected her as none had before…well, she simply couldn't bear to even think of that.

She knew he was planning to leave soon, knew his stay was only temporary, knew there could be no future for them—and she'd told herself she was braced for that. Her reaction to the near hit he'd just described let her know she wasn't as well prepared as she'd thought. And that terrified her.

His mouth was so warm on hers, so increasingly familiar. His arms were solid and secure around her, making her feel safe and protected—something she'd never sought from any man. She laid her hand against his chest, feeling the strength of his muscles beneath the thin fabric of his T-shirt. Despite the bad experiences he'd had during the past weeks, this was a man who was fully capable of taking care of himself. He'd allowed her to fuss over him, but he'd have been fine on his own. Maybe he even preferred it that way.

She slowly pulled her mouth from his and searched his face with troubled eyes. Why was she finding it so hard to resist his kisses, even though she kept reminding herself of all the reasons she should resist?

"Don't look so troubled, Serena," he said, stroking her cheek. "I'm sure it was only a bizarre accident."

"Actually, that's not what's troubling me at the moment," she murmured, all too aware of their position, his thighs beneath hers.

Catching her drift, he glanced downward. "Oh. Well, *that* was only a kiss."

"Something that seems to be happening quite a bit between us lately."

"I know." He ran his thumb across her lower lip. "You don't hear me complaining, do you?"

She gave him a stern look. "I'm not in the habit of indulging in casual affairs, Sam."

"I never supposed you were."

"I wouldn't want you to get the wrong idea because of a few impulsive kisses."

His thumb trailed across her lip again, lingering at the slight indention in the center. "I've definitely gotten ideas from those kisses, but not that one."

She leveled another stern look at him. "I'm being serious."

His crooked smile was transformed into a full-blown grin that nearly took her breath away. "Sorry,

Serena, but I really can't be intimidated by your tough-lawyer voice when you're sitting in my lap with your arms around my neck. And again, note that I'm not complaining.''

She felt her cheeks warm. When it came to this man, she really did seem to be losing her mind. She scrambled off his lap. Sam made no effort to detain her—or to hide his regret.

Pushing her hands through her disheveled hair, she drew a deep breath and tried to remember how that had gotten started this time. Oh, yes. She'd been reacting to the distress of hearing about his near hit. ''I think you should call Dan.''

''Why?''

''Why? Someone tried to run you down! Even if it was an accident, the driver left the scene without even checking to make sure you were all right. Dan should know about this.''

''I'm sure he'll contact me before long,'' Sam replied, sounding suddenly tired. ''Word gets around pretty fast in this town. Someone will tell Dan.''

She studied him disapprovingly. ''You don't seem to be taking this very seriously.''

He sighed and pushed himself out of the chair, resting his weight somewhat cautiously on his right leg. ''What do you want from me, Serena? I wasn't hit, and I didn't see the vehicle well enough to identify it. There's really nothing more I can do.''

''So you're just going to forget about it?''

''Yes, that's what I'd like to do.''

''And if someone really was trying to hurt you? Maybe the same person who tried to implicate you in the candy store robbery?''

He made a face. ''You heard about that, did you?''

"I heard. You're lucky Dan didn't throw you in jail."

"He said he doesn't make arrests based on anonymous phone calls."

"Then you're lucky he's so reasonable. Someone wanted to cause problems for you, Sam. For all we know, someone tried to cause you physical harm only hours later. I'm not at all comfortable just shrugging those incidents off as coincidental."

"I'll talk to Dan."

She had the feeling he was trying to appease her, but at least Dan would know what had happened. Or almost happened. She shivered.

Sam lay a hand on her shoulder. "I'll talk to Dan," he said again, and he sounded more sincere this time.

A new possibility occurred to her. "Is there any chance that the driver of that SUV could be one of the men who beat you up and left you in the ditch? Maybe they're trying to get rid of you now to keep you from identifying them or something."

The muscle that flexed in his jaw made her wonder if the possibility had already occurred to him. But all he said was, "Highly unlikely."

Serena scowled at him. "You're getting close-mouthed again. That means I'm asking questions you don't want to answer. What, exactly, are you keeping from me, Sam Wallace?"

Chapter Twelve

It was the moment Sam had been dreading since he'd opened his eyes in a hospital room and stared at a blank wall where his past should have been. Over and over, he'd rehearsed this scene in his mind. It had always turned out badly, with him feeling like an idiot and everyone else treating him like a freak. Everyone except Serena. In his imagination, she had always been too angry about his lies to even speak to him.

She was watching him with suspiciously narrowed eyes, waiting for him to level with her. He cleared his throat, stalling, trying to come up with the right words to tell her that she'd been kissing a guy who didn't even know his own name. For some reason, the words didn't immediately pop into his mind.

He whipped his head around when something scratched on the kitchen door behind him. "What the—"

"It's Walter." Serena studied him with a lifted eyebrow. "You were expecting another SUV?"

Chagrined by his overreaction, he turned toward the door. "I'll let him in."

She crossed her arms and watched as he moved to the back door. He didn't immediately close the door after Walter dashed in, but stood gazing out into the darkness, tempted to step into it. Perhaps he would be more comfortable out there. No identity, no past, no future—just another solitary form among the shadows.

Serena interrupted his melancholy imagery. "You were going to tell me something?"

He couldn't do it. There was no way he could explain what was wrong with him or why he had hadn't told the truth from the start. How could he justify a decision that even he recognized as completely irrational?

He had just acknowledged another uncomfortable fact about himself. Apparently, there were times when he could be a craven coward. Now, for example. "Actually, I'm a little tired," he said without looking around. "It's been...an eventful day."

"Then you can sit while you talk. I'll even make you something to eat. We can't keep putting this off, Sam."

He still had a couple of days before his self-imposed three-week deadline was up, he reminded himself. It was entirely possible that he would, somehow, manage to assemble the fragments of memory he'd recovered during the past few days into a coherent whole. It would be much easier to discuss his amnesia with Serena after he'd recovered from it, when there would be something more to tell her.

"We'll talk soon," he assured her, inching toward the doorway.

She caught his arm. "*Damn* it, Sam! I deserve better than this."

It was the one argument he couldn't refute. She was absolutely right. She deserved better than what she'd gotten from him.

He closed the door.

Serena's hand remained on his arm. "Whatever it is, whatever you're running from—maybe I can help. We can talk to Dan. If someone from your past is trying to hurt you—"

Sam quieted her by covering her hand with his free one. "You're always offering to help me," he murmured, studying the concern in her eyes. "I've never met anyone like you—at least, I don't think I have."

Typically embarrassed by the compliment, she shook her head and spoke gruffly. "Never mind that."

"No, I'm serious. Without you and Marjorie, I'd have been in a lot of trouble three weeks ago. Nowhere to go, no one to turn to, no money—not even a clean shirt to my name. There aren't many people who'd take a guy like that home and practically make him a part of the family."

Her cheeks were bright pink. "I told you, that was my mother's idea."

"Perhaps. But you were the one who sat by my side at the hospital. And you were the one who showed up with bags of clothes when I was discharged."

To avoid his eyes, she looked at their linked hands on his forearm. "Yes, well, you were going to tell me something?"

"I'm trying to tell you how much I respect you," he persisted, ignoring her discomfort and his own.

This was something he needed to say and she needed to hear before she very likely stopped speaking to him altogether. "I want you to know how much I admire your generosity and your kindness, your efficiency and your sense of responsibility to your family and your friends. You've taken on obligations you never wanted, to keep your mother from being disappointed and to make it easier for your sister to pursue her dreams—even though you make no secret that you disapprove of her choices. You've suffered over the fate of an employee you know you have to fire, and you've somehow kept your law practice going—quite successfully, from what I've heard. You've generously taken in a goofy mutt and a battered stranger—and neither of us has properly demonstrated our gratitude."

She sighed. "Are you *trying* to embarrass me?"

"I'm trying to thank you."

"You're welcome. And by the way, I think you've shown your gratitude quite adequately—with, um, all the things you've done to help out around here," she added quickly. "I've had no reason to regret bringing you home."

Because he couldn't resist, he lifted his hand to the back of her head and tugged her toward him. "Just one more," he murmured against her lips. And then he kissed her, savoring her warmth and softness, telling himself this would probably be the last time.

At least he hadn't taken further advantage of her. As many times as he had made love to her in his mind, he'd managed to behave himself when he was with her, for the most part. She could forgive a few kisses—he hoped—but anything more, under the circumstances, would be unconscionable.

She nearly shattered his precarious willpower when she slipped her arms around his neck and parted her lips. There was no way he could resist the impulse to deepen the kiss, to slide his hands down her sides, shape her slender curves beneath his palms. *One last time*.

Sam didn't want the kiss to end. He'd been completely honest with Serena—he considered her a very special woman. The kind of woman a man would want to keep in his life, he thought as he slowly lifted his head. If he *had* a life. A home. A name.

If he'd met her a few weeks earlier, before the beating that had robbed him of his memory, would it have been different between them? Would he have been free to pursue her? Would he have had the sense to do so?

He realized that she was searching his face, her eyes grave and entirely too perceptive. "You're wearing that look again," she murmured, laying a cool hand against his bruised cheek.

"What look?"

"The one that breaks my heart," she startled him by saying. And then she blinked and looked away, as if the words had slipped out without her intending them to do so.

"What is it you need to tell me, Sam?" she asked, extricating herself from his arms. "Is it something about your past?"

He drew a deep breath. "I don't have a past."

She looked puzzled. "I don't understand."

"Do you remember when I woke up in the hospital, and you spoke to me?"

"Yes, of course."

"So do I. But that's the earliest memory I have. Everything before that is a blank."

"Yes, you told us you had little memory of the beating you took. Dr. Frank said that's common after a head injury."

He was making a mess of this—as he'd known he would. "You don't understand. I have *no* memories prior to waking up in the hospital. None."

Frowning, she shook her head. "I still don't—wait a minute. You're saying you have amnesia?"

The very word made him wince. "That's the technical term for it. I can't remember anything before I woke up."

She put a hand on the counter, as if she needed the support. "But you knew your name. Your birthday."

"I made them up. I kept thinking everything would come back to me, and I wanted to be left alone while I recovered. I was afraid if I told the truth, no one would believe me. Or they *would* believe me, and they'd treat me like some sort of medical oddity."

"You made it all up." She seemed to have fixated on that admission. "You made up your name?"

"Sam was the first name that popped into my head. I had to struggle a bit to come up with Wallace."

She was looking at him as if a second head had just popped out on his shoulder. Sam crossed his arms tightly over his chest, feeling awkward and self-conscious.

"I can't believe this," she said after a pause. "It's just too..." She couldn't seem to find the word she was groping for.

"I told you it was hard to believe," he muttered, wondering what it would take to convince her if she decided the whole story was a lie.

"You mean, you woke up in the hospital with total amnesia about who you are and what you were doing there? And you haven't regained your memories during the three weeks that have passed since?"

"Technically, it will be three weeks tomorrow. And I've had glimmers of memory during those weeks, but nothing concrete. Images, a few dreams that felt real, but no names, no places."

"I can't believe this," she said again.

"I can't make you believe me, of course, but it's the truth."

"I think I need to sit down." She moved to sit in one of the chairs, resting her elbows on the table, a stunned expression on her face.

Sam took the chair opposite her, the one he'd sat in while she'd administered first aid. She seemed to need a few minutes to digest what he'd told her, so he sat in silence, absently kneading his right thigh just over his bandaged knee.

"If you have amnesia, why didn't you tell anyone? Why did you make up answers to everyone's questions to keep them from finding out the truth?"

"Look, I know it was a stupid thing to do." He shook his head. "All I can say is that I was hurting and confused—hell, maybe I was just plain scared— and I made some foolish decisions. I didn't know how people would react to the truth—and I guess I just hated admitting I was...well, brain damaged."

He watched Serena flinch in response to the term. A perfectly understandable reaction, he assured himself. Wasn't it exactly what he'd expected?

"You said you've had some flashes of memory. Like what?"

He looked at his hands. "I remember being hit as a kid. I can't picture my parents or remember anything about them, but I know what a backhand against my face feels like."

"I wondered about that," Serena murmured. When he gave her a questioning look, she explained, "You were so passionate about defending Zach from that jerk, Delbert. It seemed to go deeper than just a natural urge to protect a child."

"I did identify strongly with Zach," he admitted. "But I don't know for certain what happened to me. The memories aren't that clear."

"I doubt those were memories you wanted to recall," she said, sounding suddenly sympathetic.

He didn't want her pity any more than he wanted skepticism. "Like I said, it might not even be true."

"Were there other memories? Adult memories?"

"Disjointed images. Sitting in a restaurant. Fishing with a friend. Driving a fast car. Riding a horse. Sitting at a computer. Just…glimpses of activities that I don't know if I actually experienced or if I just imagined them."

She rubbed her temples, as if she was developing a headache. "Somewhere, there must be someone who is frantic with worry about you. Family, friends—" She swallowed. "A wife, maybe."

He focused on his left hand. "No wedding ring. No ring tan, though there's a pale strip where I must have worn a watch."

"Not every married man wears a ring."

"No. But I really don't think I'm married, Serena. If I were, surely I would know. Somehow."

"You don't even know your name," she reminded him.

This time it was Sam who winced. "I think I would know if I were married," he repeated, wishing he sounded—and felt—more certain.

She twisted her fingers on the table in front of her, her gaze focused on his face. "There must be someone who's looking for you."

"I've spent quite a bit of time at the library, searching online for any missing person report that fit my description. I've even checked police missing persons files. No matches."

Her eyebrows lifted. "You knew how to do all that?"

"Yeah. I sat down at a computer and just started searching. There was a definite sense of familiarity about sitting at a keyboard. I'm sure I've logged some computer time—I just don't know why."

"So that whole cock-and-bull story about being a drifter in search of work—"

He shrugged. "It sounded believable at the time."

She groaned and covered her eyes for a moment with her hands. "Oh, my God. You made up the story about the two muggers who robbed you and beat you up."

"It seemed to fit the way I was found. No watch or wallet or ID."

She groaned again.

"Okay, it wasn't one of my brighter decisions," he conceded with a sigh. "I guess I have to blame the concussion for that, too. By the time my mind cleared enough for me to realize how stupid and irresponsible I'd been, it seemed too late to get out of it."

"Dan's going to kill you. And then he'll lock up what's left."

He couldn't pretend to be surprised by the pessimistic prediction. It very closely resembled his own. Next time Dan took him fishing, he would likely use Sam for bait.

"We have to tell him, of course."

He reached up to rub the back of his neck. "I guess you're right."

"There's no 'guess' to it. We have to tell him. Sam, don't you understand? Someone tried to kill you three weeks ago. It could have been the same person who tried to run you down today. We're not talking about a random mugging now. Your life might still be in danger."

He'd spent too many sleepless nights trying to figure out who might have beaten him to within an inch of his life, and why. He still didn't have a clue. As for what had happened today—well, he'd like to write it off as an accident, but a niggle of doubt remained at the back of his mind. He would sure like to know if the driver had borne any resemblance to the buttoned-down stranger he'd spotted at the Independence Day celebration.

"I'll talk to Dan tomorrow," he promised.

"Tonight would be better."

He shook his head. "It can wait until office hours."

"And in the meantime? What if someone comes after you tonight?"

"Now you're letting your imagination run away with you," he chided. "I'll talk to Dan first thing in the morning, okay? Not that there's much he can do at this point."

"He can send out your description and fingerprints. Contact the media, perhaps."

Sam grimaced at the thought of his photograph in newspapers over a headline identifying him as a clueless victim.

"You'll also need to see Dr. Frank tomorrow," Serena continued. "He'll want you to see a specialist. He's a general practitioner, not a neurologist. He'll probably send you to Little Rock. I doubt that our little hospital has the equipment or the expertise to treat a case like this."

"'A case like this?'" he repeated in a carefully neutral tone.

"Total amnesia," she clarified. "It has to be quite rare. Dr. Frank's probably never seen a case that—"

"I'd really appreciate it if you'd stop referring to me as a case," he said irritably.

Serena bit her lip. "I'm sorry. I—"

"Forget it." He stood, ignoring a twinge of pain from his stiffening knee. "I'm the one who owes the apology. To you *and* your mother. You both deserved the truth from me, and all I did was take advantage of your kindness. I'll clear out tomorrow—and wherever I end up, I'll make sure you're repaid as soon as possible."

Serena rolled her eyes. "Would you stop being a stiff-necked idiot? You aren't clearing out until we know you have someplace to go. And you haven't taken advantage of us. You've more than earned your pay at the diner and you've got the house and lawn looking better than they have since Dad died."

She didn't sound furious, he thought with a touch

of surprise. Exasperated, maybe. Bewildered by his actions, certainly. But not as angry as he'd expected.

Maybe she just hadn't had enough time to really think about what he'd done.

"Sit back down," she ordered, pushing herself to her feet. "I'll make us some dinner."

"That's really not—"

"I'm hungry," she said simply. "I'm sure you are, too. And we still need to talk."

He sat slowly. "I don't suppose you want to sit in my lap again while we talk."

It was a weak joke, and poorly timed. The look Serena gave him made him sink into the chair with his mouth tightly closed, telling himself to shut up while he was—well, not ahead, perhaps, but at least not too far behind.

Either Sam had been hungrier than he'd admitted, or he used food to avoid conversation during the dinner Serena had thrown together. She suspected the latter. Of course, she didn't say much during the meal, either. She didn't really know what to say.

She was still struggling to accept the fact that Sam—the only name she had for him—had amnesia. Seeing her beside his hospital bed was his earliest memory. Everything he'd told her since had been sheer fabrication.

He could be married. Every time he'd kissed her, he might have been betraying another woman. She should be relieved that they'd gone no further than a few heated kisses. But, strangely enough, it wasn't relief she felt.

Abused boy. Obviously well-educated man. Familiar with computers, yet comfortable waiting tables in a small-town diner. A man found beaten senseless in a ditch. A man with a kind heart, a wry humor, a likable manner and an overdeveloped sense of self-sufficiency. Who *was* he?

"You said you've been having dreams," she said when he seemed to be nearing completion of his meal. "What are they like?"

Sam set his fork down. "Faces. Voices. Nothing solid."

"The same faces and voices? Or are they different every time?"

His expression was distant, as if he were looking into one of those dreams as they spoke. "Sometimes the same. Sometimes different."

She found herself speaking softly, as if to keep from rousing him too completely. "Are they good dreams?"

"For the most part. Usually, the people I see are laughing. Talking. Playing games."

"That sounds pleasant."

"Mostly, yes."

She noticed that he rubbed his leg as he spoke, indicating that the fresh wounds he'd received were bothering him. "Do you want something for pain?"

His hand stilled. "No. I'm fine."

Knowing him too well to argue with that particular tone, she returned to her questioning. "You said most of the dreams are pleasant. What about the ones that aren't?"

His grimace let her know she'd stepped into a sensitive area. "The people in those don't laugh."

He didn't seem to want to talk about the bad

dreams—and she supposed she couldn't blame him for that. "There has to be a clue somewhere about what happened to you," she murmured. "Dan said he searched the ditch where you were found very thoroughly, but maybe he missed something."

Sam shook his head. "I've looked. That's what I'd been doing the last time Walter got out."

It had been the day he'd fixed the fence. She'd fussed at him for walking all the way down to the lake so soon after recovering from his injuries. She'd had no way of knowing, of course, that he'd been searching for his identity.

"We'll find out who you are," she reiterated. "With Dan and Dr. Frank's help, we'll get your answers."

He looked away, but not before she recognized the expression in his eyes. She knew now why she'd thought of it as his lost look. He *was* lost.

The thought of what he'd been going through made her heart ache for him. It was bad enough that he'd been in such terrible shape from the beating. But to wake up confused and hurting, surrounded by strangers, his memories gone—it must have been terrifying.

She was still stunned that he'd decided to try to conceal his amnesia rather than ask for help—but who knew how she would react under the same circumstances? Like Sam, she disliked being dependent on others, hated being sick and at the mercy of the medical profession. She preferred to solve her own problems, take care of herself—and her family, for that matter. Was it entirely inconceivable that she might have reacted much as Sam had? Stalled for time while she tried to solve her predicament in her own way?

Okay, maybe she wouldn't have handled it exactly the way Sam had. But she could—sort of—understand how he'd felt.

"There's some pecan pie in the fridge," she said, deciding he needed to talk about something else for a while. "Mother made it earlier this week. Would you like some?"

"No, thanks." He glanced at the door. "Actually, I think I'd like to go soak in a hot bath before I stiffen up any more than I already have."

"Are you sure you don't want to take something for pain?"

"I've got some aspirin in the guest house. I'll take a couple of those before I turn in."

She followed him to the door. "If you need anything during the night, just let me know, okay?"

"Anything?"

Because his lopsided grin was the one that usually preceded a kiss, her knees weakened. She stiffened them with an effort. "You know what I mean."

He gave an exaggerated sigh. "Yes, I'm afraid I do. I'll see you tomorrow, Serena."

"We'll go see Dan first thing in the morning."

"We?"

"You might very well find yourself in need of a lawyer."

He chuckled wryly. "Or maybe Dan will need the lawyer—after he strangles me."

"That's another possibility," she conceded.

"Good night, Serena."

"Good night—Sam."

The momentary hesitation before his name didn't escape him. He gave a funny, faintly apologetic little shrug, then let himself out. Serena closed the door behind him with a sigh. And then she rested her head against the wood, a dull ache throbbing in her temples.

She'd thought the man Kara had fallen for was unsuitable because he was too young and too impractical. But at least Pierce knew who he was, where he'd come from.

Kara might be the adventurous sister, but Serena seemed to be the one currently on a path to certain disaster.

Chapter Thirteen

The chains supporting the rose-garden swing creaked when Sam sank into it. Other than the crickets, frogs and night birds in the woods behind the neighborhood, the creaking was the only sound to disturb the stillness of the night. He caught himself listening for revving car engines, wailing sirens, raised voices—even gunshots. What kind of life had he led before that had caused him to think of those sounds as an inextricable part of the night?

He closed his eyes and savored the quiet peacefulness. Was it possible that he'd once preferred those other, half-remembered noises to this? If so, how could a blow to the head have changed his entire personality so radically?

It had been another dream that had disturbed his sleep and brought him outside to try to clear his mind with rose-scented night air. It wasn't one of the good dreams this time—the ones filled with echoes of laughter and sensations of warmth. This had been a dream he'd had before, and one that always left him feeling empty and depressed.

Who was the woman who cried in those dreams? He could almost picture her now—young, fresh-faced, pretty in a wholesome sort of way. Yet her face had been reddened and tear-streaked, her expression miserable. And though he couldn't remember who she was or what his connection was to her, he knew somehow that she was real—and that he had caused her tears.

Someone who had loved him? He'd tried to focus on his own feelings toward her in the dreams, identifying only a vague sense of affection and sympathy. And guilt. Definite guilt. He had little doubt that he'd been the cause of her misery, though that was the only fact he knew for certain.

Who *was* she? And who was *he*, that he had hurt her so badly?

"Are you in pain?"

Serena's quiet question made him open his eyes. He hadn't heard her approach, which indicated he'd been completely lost in his thoughts. She stood in front of the swing, bathed in the glow of the summer moon. Her hair was tousled around her unpainted face. She wore a tank top and shorts, leaving quite a bit of creamy skin bare. She was as much a part of this place as the roses and the night birds, a vital part of the peace and the charm. He was the outsider here.

He remembered that early-regained memory of Brigadoon, the magical village suspended in time whose residents were unable to leave. His initial fear had been that he would be trapped here. Now he dreaded the inevitable time when he would have to go.

"Sam? Are you okay?"

He made an effort to smile. "I'm fine. Just having another night when I can't sleep. I hope I didn't wake you."

"No, I was awake. My grandmother used to call these hoot owl spells—nights when your eyes just won't stay closed."

"Yeah. Guess I'm having a hoot owl spell."

"So am I. I can't seem to turn off my thoughts."

"What are you thinking about so seriously?"

"You," she said after only a momentary hesitation.

He stood, leaving the swing swaying behind him. He'd donned the gym shorts and a T-shirt to come outside, so he had no pockets in which to shove his hands. Instead, he crossed his arms over his chest and tucked his hands into his elbows in an attempt to keep them out of trouble. "Have you come up with any new theories?"

"That isn't what I've been thinking about."

"Oh?" He studied her face, trying to understand her mood.

"I've been thinking about how much we've enjoyed having you here," she said quietly. "How much a part of our lives—of our town—you've become in such a short time. Less than a month, yet in some ways it seems like you've been here much longer than that."

He thought of the people he'd met in this town, the ones he already knew by name and reputation. He could hardly go out now without running into someone he knew from the diner or through Serena and Marjorie. Less than a month—yes, it was a bit hard to believe.

"When you find out who you are—when your memory returns—you'll probably go back to your old life." She sighed lightly. "That's the way it should be, of course, but—"

"But?"

"I—we'll miss you," she whispered.

He swallowed. "As you said, I've only been here three weeks."

She gave a little shrug. "A lot can happen in three weeks."

He had to agree with that. A lot *could* happen in three weeks. Lives could change. Friends could come and go. People could fall in love.

Now where had *that* thought come from? He wasn't the type to wax romantic—at least, he was pretty sure he wasn't. He didn't believe in love at first sight or whirlwind courtships or other such foolishness—at least, he didn't think he did. And he sure as hell didn't want to be responsible for putting a look on Serena's face like the one he'd seen in the eyes of the woman in his dreams.

"You'd better get some sleep," he said, looking at the house, knowing if he looked at her face he would be a goner. "Tomorrow could be a long day."

"Tomorrow could be our *last* day."

He supposed that could be true. There was a distinct possibility that someone would want to lock him up tomorrow—Dan in a jail or Dr. Frank in a psych ward, he thought with a grim attempt at humor. "Yes, well…"

Their eyes met. Hers were filled with emotions he couldn't quite interpret.

He shouldn't have looked at her. He'd been holding his own against his libido, reminding himself of all the reasons he should keep his distance. But looking at Serena with her eyes gleaming in the moonlight, her lips slightly parted—hell, he wasn't a statue.

He wasn't sure which of them moved first. Maybe it was simultaneous—he opened his arms, she stepped into them. Maybe it was a force neither of them could resist that brought their mouths together. By the time the kiss ended, Sam had forgotten every reason they shouldn't be doing this—and he had the impression he wasn't the only one suffering from amnesia this time.

They were halfway to the guest house when he surfaced enough to regain a shred of common sense. "Serena, this really isn't a good idea."

"No," she agreed, but she didn't stop walking.

"I wouldn't want either of us to have regrets."

She put her hand on the doorknob to the guest house and looked over her shoulder at him. "Everyone has regrets. You learn to live with them."

It wasn't the most reassuring thing she could have said. Certainly not the most poetic. But he supposed it was as good an argument as any.

He followed her inside when she opened the door.

Serena wasn't acting on impulse, exactly. Sometime during the hours when she'd tried to sleep, she'd realized that she didn't want to let it end with Sam simply leaving—or being led away—to find his past. She wanted him to carry a few memories of her with him—and she wanted a few of her own to reminisce about in the future.

She'd reflected before that few men like Sam ever found their way to Edstown. She didn't expect another to come along anytime soon. She remembered something Kara had said during their conversation earlier that evening. "The real regrets would have come if I'd chosen *not* to take a chance on love."

Despite Serena's usual almost obsessive caution, Kara wasn't the only one who could take chances occasionally.

It was only a few steps across the tiny living room to the equally small bedroom. The tousled queen-size bed took up most of the floor space. Serena paused beside it, turning to face Sam. The three-way lamp on the nightstand had been left on, its bulb so dim that it barely made a difference. Sam's face was partially shadowed, making him look as mysterious and enigmatic as she now knew him to be.

She should probably be nervous at this point. She should at least have a few qualms or misgivings. But she didn't. Whatever happened tomorrow when the truth about Sam's condition came out, she would always have this night.

He took a step toward her, his mouth so close to hers she could feel his breath like a warm night breeze against her skin. But he kept his hands at his sides. "It just occurred to me," he murmured, "that there's something you forgot to buy when you shopped for me. I'm sure you didn't realize we'd be needing protection, but it's rather inconvenient at the—"

She pulled a hand out of her shorts pocket, letting the dim light reflect from the shiny plastic packets in her palm.

Letting his words trail away, Sam lifted his gaze from her hand to her face. She couldn't quite read his expression, but there was approval in his voice when he said, "Never mind."

She tossed the packets on the bed. "I thought you'd realized by now that I don't believe in taking risks."

He lifted his hands to clasp her hips, holding her lightly against him. "You don't consider this a risk?"

She slipped her arms around his neck. "I consider this a temporary lapse in judgment," she replied candidly. "I understand everyone has them occasionally."

"Then let's make it worthwhile," he murmured, and crushed her mouth beneath his.

Even as they sank together to the bed, Serena knew exactly what had clinched this decision for her. It was that air of deep-seated loneliness about him. The sadness in his bright blue eyes that had caused LuWanda to speculate that he'd survived a tragedy of some sort. Looking out from her bedroom window, she had seen him sitting alone in the garden swing, and her heart had ached in response to the downward curve of his shoulders. He needed someone tonight. He needed *her*.

Whatever he faced tomorrow, perhaps it would be a bit easier for him after tonight. He would know that for now, at least, he wasn't alone.

It had not been wise of her to fall in love with a stranger, but she would worry about that later. She had more important things to concentrate on now.

The few clothes they'd worn were easily shed. Seeming to understand that Serena needed to take this at her own pace, Sam was relatively patient while she explored him. She pressed her lips softly to assorted scars and scrapes, brushed her fingers gently over the fresh bandage on his knee, ached in sympathy for every twinge of pain he'd suffered. And then she reveled in the strength of the lean muscles beneath his bruised skin. He might be a bit battered and confused, but there was no doubt he was a strong, vibrant male in his prime—and Serena was woman enough to appreciate that.

So there, Kara.

Sam drew her mouth to his, driving all thoughts of her sister—all coherent thought, actually—from her mind. He'd obviously been patient for as long as he could. He shifted her onto her back, giving him the freedom to do some exploring of his own. His hands and lips raced over her body, pausing here and there to elicit gasps of startled pleasure from her. There were obviously some things he hadn't forgotten at all....

He kissed her breasts, her stomach, her thighs, her knees—and then kissed her with an intimacy that stole whatever breath she'd had left. By the time he returned to her mouth, her limbs were rubbery, her skin almost overly sensitized, her breathing raggedly uneven. A fire burned somewhere deep inside her, its heat almost unbearable. She squirmed from the intensity of it, craving relief even as she relished the sensations.

She tried to help him don the protection she'd provided, but her hands were shaking too hard to provide much assistance. That startled her. She rarely allowed herself to be overwhelmed with emotion.

His eyes locked with hers as he held himself poised above her. Battling a sudden attack of nerves, she searched his face, trying to read his thoughts. In so many ways he was still a stranger to her. She knew so little about him. So few solid facts. She didn't even know his name. And yet, in some ways, she felt as if she knew him very well. And the characteristics she had observed in him during the past three weeks had been nothing but admirable.

She couldn't believe he was a man who didn't deserve her respect...her love. Whether he was free to accept it—well, that was something else she would have to worry about later. With a heartfelt mental apology to anyone who might be hurt by her selfish actions, she reached out to pull Sam to her.

Murmuring her name, he gathered her close, his mouth covering hers as he joined their bodies in one smooth thrust. She arched to meet him with a muffled cry of pleasure.

There were no thoughts about who he was or where he'd come from. For this night he was just Sam, the man who had come into her life so dramatically, so unexpectedly and had so effortlessly illustrated everything she had been missing. Funny. She hadn't been fully aware that there *was* anything missing until she'd met him.

Even as she threw herself into the maelstrom of emotions his lovemaking evoked in her, she was aware of a slight niggling of fear at the back of her mind that after he left, she would be all too aware of the emptiness he left behind.

The dream was different this time. The woman he'd seen before was in it, but she wasn't crying. She was laughing, as were the people who surrounded her. Men and women of about his own age, their faces as familiar to him as his own, their identities as lost to him. They were laughing, talking, gathered around a table—playing a card game, perhaps? He could almost hear their voices, almost catch their names. Did someone say the name Michael? Was someone called Kelly?

One of them, a man, spoke to him in the dream. Sam almost recognized him—was he the same man he'd imagined at the other end of a fishing boat?

Tanned, brown-haired, blue-eyed, lanky. *Shane*. The guy's name was Shane. Sam could almost hear him speaking in a lazy, deep drawl, calling him by name. The name Sam—no, wait, it wasn't Sam. It was—

"Sam?"

A woman's voice this time, disturbing his sleep, making him frown and try harder to hang on to the images.

"Sam?" More insistent this time.

He opened his eyes, blinking in the darkness, his mind filled with echoes of other voices. "What?"

Serena was leaning over him, holding the sheet to her breasts with one hand. "You were dreaming."

"I know." He rubbed a hand over his gritty eyes.

"I didn't know whether I should wake you, but you seemed…agitated."

"It's okay."

"You were saying something. It sounded like…" She hesitated, then whispered, "Jane. I think you were saying the name Jane. Do you…do you remember who she is?"

"It wasn't Jane. It was Shane." He could see the guy's face again even as he repeated, "Shane."

"A man?" Serena sounded both relieved and puzzled. "You remember a man named Shane?"

"Sort of. I don't know for certain, but I think he's a friend. Maybe…a brother."

"A brother?" She sat up straighter, tucking the sheet beneath her arms. "Sam, this could be important. What else did you remember? His last name? Your own?"

He shook his head, his thoughts starting to clear, the images beginning to fade. "They weren't clear memories. Just flashes, like I've had before. And as for the guy—Shane—I don't really know who he is. Probably not a brother. I said that only because he felt like someone who's been a part of my life for a long time.''

"A brother or a friend. Either way you know there are people out there somewhere who care about you. Who are missing you, maybe looking for you. There has to be a way to find them.''

His laugh sounded hollow even to him. "You seem rather anxious to get rid of me.''

"You know better than that,'' she chided softly, then added, "I would think you'd be more anxious to find the answers yourself.''

He reached up to stroke her tumbled hair, smoothing it away from her face. "I rather enjoy being Sam Wallace,'' he murmured. "I'm not so sure I'd like the guy I was before.''

She rested a hand on his chest, just over his heart. "I don't know what happened to you, or how you ended up here the way you did, but there's one thing I do know. Whatever your name is, you're a good man. An honest man, with a kind heart and a deep sense of honor. You've suffered hardships, but they've only made you stronger. You remember friends, which means you know how to be a friend yourself. I don't think you have anything to fear about facing your past.''

She didn't know about the crying woman, of course. The one he'd somehow hurt so badly. But her faith in him touched him immeasurably. "I hope you're right,'' he said.

"I'm right.'' She spoke with a certainty he envied. "I can't believe amnesia would change your entire personality.''

Maybe not. But it could certainly change his circumstances. He was certain that Sam Wallace's life was very different from the one he'd led before. For one thing, his life before hadn't included Serena. How could it have been better than this?

Because the thought of going back to a life without her depressed him, he reached out to pull her into his arms, holding her tightly, reminding himself that at least they had the rest of this night. He didn't want to waste a minute of it.

She let go of the sheet to wrap her arms around him, clinging to him as if her thoughts were similar to his. As their mouths met, Sam decided that he'd be perfectly content to remain right where they were. No past. No future. No doubts or uncertainties. Only this. He couldn't imagine finding anything better, no matter what he learned tomorrow.

Before she slipped out of his bed at dawn, Sam convinced Serena to delay their trip to Dan's office until after his shift at the diner. He assured her that Marjorie needed him that day and that the big confession to Dan could wait a few hours.

Serena made him promise not to tell Marjorie anything yet. Not until after he'd been thoroughly checked over by Dr. Frank, anyway. "Mother's grown so fond of you," she explained. "She'll worry herself sick if we don't assure her that you're fine except for your memory loss."

Though Sam still felt guilty for the lies he'd told, it wasn't hard for Serena to convince him to put off telling Marjorie the truth. He wasn't quite ready to face the certain disillusionment in her kind eyes.

Telling her he'd meet her at the police station after

the diner closed, he kissed Serena at his door, then watched her hurry to the main house where she hoped to slip into her room without her mother being aware that she'd been gone. The sky was just beginning to lighten in the east. He'd had very little sleep, but he certainly had no regrets about that. He felt totally revitalized by the hours he'd spent in Serena's arms.

Breakfast at the diner was actually even busier than he'd expected. There'd been another fire during the night, a recently vacated rent house this time. The word *arson* was being used quite a bit. The citizens of Edstown were concerned that a firebug had moved into their area. Justine spent the morning complaining to anyone who would listen about the deteriorating state of society.

By the time the lunchtime crowd arrived, news of another crime had spread. Another business had been broken into during the night, a pawnshop this time. The break-in hadn't been discovered until the owner had arrived to open his shop just before ten, finding that guns, jewelry and money had been taken during the night. He had a rudimentary security system, but it had been circumvented. "I told Herman a long time ago that his security system was obsolete," one of the diners told Sam during a discussion of the crime. "These new crooks are too smart to be put off by a couple of trip wires and motion lights."

"An arson *and* a burglary," Justine fretted when she and Sam crossed paths in the kitchen as they collected orders. "The world really is going to hell in a handbasket."

And she was thoroughly enjoying the scandal that ensued, Sam thought with a smothered smile. Residents of small towns had their own ways of finding entertainment, gossip being among the favored choices.

It was still an hour before closing time when two uniformed police officers entered the diner and asked to speak to Sam.

Aware that every eye in the place was focused on him, Sam thanked Justine for summoning him, then curiously approached the officers, who waited just inside the doorway. Had Serena already talked to Dan? Surely she wouldn't have done so without waiting for him. "Is there something I can do for you, officers?"

"You're Sam Wallace?" the taller of the two men inquired.

He wasn't quite sure how to respond, so he merely nodded.

"We'd like to request that you accompany us to the police station. Chief Meadows would like to speak to you."

Frowning, Sam looked from one impassive face to the other. "Mind if I ask what this is about?"

The officers exchanged a glance, and then the same one replied, "The chief wants to ask you some questions concerning a crime that was committed last night."

"The arson or the break-in?" Sam asked in resignation. Apparently, the anonymous accuser had been busy again. This was just what he needed today.

"Please come with us, Mr. Wallace."

"Am I under arrest?"

"No, sir. The chief would simply like to ask you some questions at this point. He sent us to escort you because he's aware that you lack transportation."

"Is there a problem here, Sam?" Marjorie looked

concerned as she joined them, her gaze darting from Sam to the police officers.

"Looks like I'm going to have to take the rest of the day off, Marjorie," he told her. "It's nothing to worry about. Dan just wants to ask me some questions."

"Has he found a lead on the men who beat you up?"

Sam shot a warning look at the cops. "I'm not sure. I suppose he'll tell me what it's about when I get there. He sent these two gentlemen to give me a lift."

The answer seemed to satisfy her for the moment. "Call me if you need a ride home or anything," she said. "I hope Dan has some good news for you."

"Er, thanks." Sam turned toward the exit. "Shall we go, officers?"

One of them opened the door and led the way out. The other followed closely at Sam's heels. Sam didn't remember if he'd ever been arrested, but he had a feeling it would feel very much like this.

The police station was in the newer part of town, several miles from the diner. The ride was made in near silence, the officers making little attempt at conversation and Sam having nothing in particular to say. Upon arrival, he was taken directly to Dan's office, where Dan waited behind an oak desk. "Not a bad police station for such a small town," Sam commented as he entered.

Dan's smile didn't reach his eyes as he waved Sam into one of the two chairs on the other side of his desk. "It's only two years old. The old police station was crumbling around our ears."

Sam glanced at the two officers who'd followed him

in. "Thanks for sending the car, by the way. Very thoughtful of you."

Dan glanced at his subordinates, apparently sending them silent orders. They left without comment, leaving the door open behind them.

"Very well trained for small-town cops," Sam drawled approvingly.

The hint of sarcasm did not pass over Dan's head. He gave Sam a look, but said only, "One of them is my cousin. The other is the mayor's nephew. You can save the nepotism jokes until later."

Deciding they'd danced around long enough, Sam leaned forward in his seat and looked directly into the chief's eyes. "What's this about, Dan?"

Dan leaned back in his chair, rubbing his neck. "I suppose you heard we had another eventful night."

"A probable arson and a pawnshop robbery. I heard. Let me guess—you've had another anonymous phone call about me."

"Not this time." Dan opened a bottom drawer on his desk. "This time I'm afraid we have some evidence."

"What are you talking about?"

Tossing a plastic bag on the desktop, Dan asked somberly, "Does that look familiar to you?"

The bag held the cap Dan had given Sam. "Where did you get that?"

Dan's expression was grim when he answered. "It was found under a counter in the pawnshop this morning, beside a couple of items the thief apparently dropped on his way out."

Sam was shaking his head before Dan even finished speaking. "Uh-uh. No way. I wasn't there, Dan."

The chief only looked at him, his stern face unrevealing.

"Surely you don't believe I had anything to do with the pawnshop robbery."

"I'll be honest with you, Sam, I'm not so sure what to believe about you right now. There are too many things about you that just don't add up. Now you've been linked to two burglaries. Sure, the anonymous call seemed suspicious, but now—well, this *is* the cap I gave you."

"It's my cap," Sam conceded, "but I wasn't wearing it last night."

"When was the last time you remember seeing it?"

Sam tried to think. So much had happened during the past twenty-four hours. "Yesterday afternoon. I was wearing it after work."

"You visited the pawnshop?"

"No. I stopped by the library for a couple hours, then just walked around downtown for a while. Then the SUV almost hit me and I..." He frowned. "It must have fallen off then."

"Yes, I heard about that. Red Tucker's convinced someone tried to kill you yesterday."

"Red has a vivid imagination," Sam reminded Dan as he tried to remember whether he'd seen the cap after diving out of the vehicle's path. Things had gotten pretty hectic then—Red had rushed up to him, then taken him home, there'd been the tell-all discussion with Serena and then the rest of the night. Was it any wonder the cap had been the last thing on his mind?

"We'll talk about that near miss in a minute. Right now, I'd like to know where you were around four this morning."

In paradise, Sam could have answered, but what he said was, ''I was in bed.''

''And there's no way you can prove that, I suppose.''

''Actually, there is,'' Serena said from the doorway. ''I was with him.''

Chapter Fourteen

Suppressing a sigh, Sam turned in his chair to look at Serena. Since it was well before the time when they'd agreed to meet here, he could only assume that someone—probably Marjorie—had called her. And now she was here, a combative set to her jaw, a gleam of temper in her eyes as she glared at Dan. He had a feeling that all hell was about to break loose in the chief's office.

Dan must have thought he'd misunderstood Serena's words. "What are you doing here?"

"Don't yell at Hazel for not announcing me—I told her you were expecting me." Serena walked briskly into the room, looking every inch the lawyer in her emerald green business suit, her hair pinned into a twist at the back of her head. "What's going on here, Dan? Why did two uniformed officers pick Sam up at the diner? Couldn't whatever you wanted to talk to him about have waited until after he finished his shift to save him from the possible embarrassment of gossip and speculation?''

''My reasons are between me and Sam—unless you're here as his counsel?''

''Does he need an attorney?'' she asked coolly.

''Dan thinks he has evidence that I robbed the pawnshop last night,'' Sam informed her. ''The cap he gave me was found under a counter there this morning.''

''Nonsense.'' Serena sank gracefully into the chair beside Sam's. ''Dan's not stupid enough to believe you'd pull a stunt like that, no matter what circumstantial evidence he found.''

Dan scowled. ''Damn it, Serena.''

She lifted an eyebrow. ''I was merely stating my confidence in your intelligence. I'm sure you won't do or say anything to change my opinion.''

''This is the second break-in in two days Sam's been connected to,'' he argued. ''I would really lack intelligence—not to mention professional competence—if I failed to follow up on that.''

''The only connection Sam had to the first break-in was an accusatory phone call from someone who wouldn't even give you a name. This time you have a cap, but Sam has an alibi—me.''

Dan cleared his throat. ''The pawnshop was most likely robbed sometime between three and four this morning. Sam claims he was in bed at that time.''

Serena met his eyes steadily. ''He was. And I was with him from about midnight to just before dawn. He didn't leave the guest house and he did *not* rob the pawnshop.''

Looking suddenly uncomfortable, Dan shuffled papers on his desk. "Er—"

"Look at me, Dan Meadows," Serena ordered, sounding to Sam rather amusingly like her mother. "Do you really think I would lie to protect someone who could be involved in a crime?"

He gave a heavy sigh. "No. If you say he was with you, then I have no choice but to believe you."

"Exactly. I've never lied to you before, and I'm not doing so now. Sam wasn't involved—and I'm frankly amazed that you ever had any doubts about that."

Dan scowled. "Well, what was I supposed to think when I found the cap I gave him under a pile of evidence?"

"If you'd used your head, you'd have realized that someone was trying to falsely implicate him—first with an anonymous phone call and now with planted evidence."

"You make that sound like a perfectly reasonable conclusion to jump to."

"It's so obvious." Waving a hand to dismiss any other possibility, Serena turned to Sam. "When did you lose the cap?"

"Probably when I jumped out of the way of that SUV on Main Street yesterday. I'm pretty sure I was wearing the cap before, but I don't remember seeing it afterward."

"So when Red helped you into his truck and brought you home, the cap was left lying on the sidewalk."

"Apparently."

"So anyone could have picked it up and carried it with them into the pawnshop during the night."

He nodded.

"Do you remember anyone who witnessed the incident, other than Red?"

He frowned. "Yeah. Delbert Farley was there. I was actually on my way across the street to speak to him when I heard the SUV."

When Serena's eyes widened, he held up a admonitory hand. As much as he disliked Farley, he was reluctant to cast aspersions without evidence unlike whoever was trying to implicate him. "As you just pointed out, *anyone* could have found the cap."

But Serena had whirled to face Dan again. "How closely have you looked at Farley? What are the odds he's involved in those break-ins?"

"You think that possibility hasn't occurred to me?" Dan was beginning to sound rather peevish. And then he rubbed his temple. "I'll look again."

"I think you should. And now that we've cleared up any doubt of Sam's innocence," she added firmly, "there's something else we need to discuss."

Dan glanced at his watch. "You'll have to make it quick. I've got an arson and a break-in to investigate— and those on top of the workload left over from yesterday."

"This isn't going to make your day any better," Sam predicted resignedly.

Dan muttered what might have been a curse beneath his breath. "Am I going to need a cup of coffee for this?"

"You might well need a stiff drink for this," Sam replied.

Dan groaned and punched a button on his desk intercom. "Hazel, do we have any fresh coffee out there?"

"Just made a pot. How many cups do you need?"

"Three," he replied when Serena and Sam nodded in response to his questioning look. And then he leaned back in his chair, drew an exaggeratedly deep breath and said, "Okay. Let me have it."

Serena was exhausted by the time she prepared for bed that evening. It had been a very long day after a near-sleepless night. Not that she lamented the lack of sleep. She knew she should be castigating herself for giving in to her hormones last night—but she couldn't seem to work up any genuine regret. Last night had been one of the more memorable experiences of her life. How could she regret that?

She stepped to her bedroom window, looking out at the guest house. There were no lights burning in the windows. Maybe Sam was getting some sleep. It had been a very long day for him, too.

The meeting with Dan had been as difficult as she and Sam had predicted. Dan had been stunned and then steamed that Sam had concealed his amnesia behind a made-up tale of a mugging. Serena had reminded Dan that Sam had acted while still confused, disoriented and in pain, barely accountable for his actions. After dryly reminding Serena that she wasn't arguing a case in front of a jury, Dan had promised to get started immediately on the search for Sam's real identity.

Serena had driven Sam to Dr. Frank's clinic after they left the police station. She'd called to set up an appointment. After hearing what the problem was, Dr. Frank had immediately agreed to work Sam into his already busy schedule. Like Dan, the doctor had reprimanded Sam for keeping quiet, this time for medical reasons. He had done a very thorough examination and then had set up appointments with specialists in Little Rock for Monday, pulling every string he had to get Sam in that quickly. He'd seemed encouraged that Sam was having flashes of memory and dreams that seemed meaningful, but he was obviously concerned that the extensive memory loss had lasted so long.

"He seemed to believe me," Sam had told Serena on the way home.

"Well, of course he believed you. Why wouldn't he?"

Though Sam hadn't come up with an answer, he still seemed bemused by the doctor's acceptance of his peculiar tale.

Marjorie's first reaction to hearing about Sam's amnesia had been exactly what Serena had expected. She'd been horrified, certain that Sam was suffering from a terrible injury that put him in imminent danger of dying. Sam and Serena had assured her that Dr. Frank had pronounced him in generally good health, considering everything.

Even though Sam had apologized profusely for deceiving her, Marjorie hadn't seemed to find his repentance necessary. "I'm just sorry," she had said, "that you've had to go through this alone. I wish you'd felt comfortable sharing it with us, but of course we were strangers to you. You needed time to grow comfortable with us."

Serena could tell that Marjorie's warm sympathy only made Sam feel guiltier. Since she thought a little guilt was justified, Serena had remained quiet. He really should have leveled with them sooner, even though she understood him well enough now to know why he hadn't.

Marjorie had insisted that Sam stay for dinner. If

she'd noticed the long, expressive looks Serena and Sam had exchanged during the meal, she'd given no sign of it.

It had been Marjorie who'd commented on how tired Sam looked after dinner, pointing out the dark circles under his eyes and the drawn look around his mouth. "You've been worrying too much and trying too hard to regain your memories. You need to get some sleep. And take tomorrow off if you'd like to sleep in," she added.

Serena hadn't been surprised when Sam immediately rejected that offer. "I have to be gone Monday," he said. "I'll be at work tomorrow."

Marjorie hadn't argued. Like Serena, she'd learned to recognize when Sam had made up his mind.

Marjorie had seemed to want to talk after Sam left, but Serena had also claimed exhaustion and made her escape. She needed to be alone with her thoughts for a while. She needed to try to sort out her emotions— not that she was making much headway. Perhaps because she was a bit afraid to define her emotions where Sam was concerned.

She hoped he was able to sleep. She wasn't. She was too aware of Sam sleeping in the guest house. She would love to be with him now, to sleep in his arms again. But it was just as well she wasn't there, she tried to convince herself. She wouldn't want to get used to being with him when she knew that he could be gone at any time.

She was about to turn away from the window when her attention was caught by a shadowy movement in the rose garden. She looked closer and saw Sam standing there looking at her window, his face just visible in the glow of the security lights.

Stay where you are, Serena.

He looked lonely, she thought, resting a hand against the window.

Don't do it, Serena. Quit while you're ahead.

He didn't sit on the swing. He just stood there, gazing at her—and she knew he saw her looking at him. She told herself he wasn't really sending her a silent invitation—but she knew he was. And then she told herself that, even if he was, she didn't have to accept—but she knew better than that, too.

She turned away from the window, but only to move toward the door. If she was going to have regrets eventually, she might as well follow Sam's advice and make them worthwhile.

They overslept. Had the rising sun not glinted in Serena's eyes, they might have slept until noon without stirring. She sat up with a gasp, her eyes turning instantly to the clock on the nightstand. "Oh, cripes." She started to roll out of the bed.

Sam's arm fell over her, holding her in place. "What's the rush?"

"It's almost six. Mother will be leaving for the diner in half an hour."

He nuzzled her cheek, his morning beard scratchy against her skin. "Think she's noticed you're missing yet?"

"No. I sometimes sleep in on Saturdays. My bedroom door is closed, so she probably thinks I'm still in bed."

"She's right, isn't she?" His lips grazed her collarbone. "You're just not in *your* bed."

"Sam, be serious." She tried to sound stern, though she tilted her head to give him better access to her throat. Her fingers speared into his thick golden hair. "She's going to be expecting you to meet her at the car, as you do every morning. You're the one who told her you intend to work today."

Planting a chain of kisses from her throat to her breastbone, he murmured, "It doesn't take me long to get ready."

"If you're late, she'll worry and come looking for you."

"I won't be late." His mouth was warm and damp against her nipple, almost clearing her mind of coherent thought.

Her fingers tightening reflexively in his hair, she made a determined effort to concentrate. "I'll wait here until after you and Mother leave for the diner, and then I'll slip back into the house. With any luck, Mother will never realize I wasn't there all night."

"You're afraid she'll ground you?" he asked, lazy amusement in his morning-rough voice.

"No, of course not. She treats me as an adult—I just think it would be easier for all of us if we don't let this get too complicated."

"'This?'" he repeated, his hands doing incredibly wicked and wonderful things beneath the sheets.

He was obviously in a good mood this morning. "You know what I mean," she said. "I'm trying to plan what we're going to do."

"You sound just like Molly when she's hatching one of her schemes," Sam teased. "Always more complicated than it needs to be."

Serena went very still. "Molly?"

He was still concentrating on her breasts. "Mmm," he said absently. "Shane's little—"

"Shane's little what?" she asked with quiet urgency.

He lifted his head with a frown. "What?"

She pushed herself into a sitting position, pulling the sheet up with her. "You said something about Molly. Shane's little...?"

He rubbed a hand over his face. "I think I was going to say sister."

"Do you remember them?"

"I—" Rolling onto his back, he stared at the ceiling. "No. Maybe I did remember them for a moment, but it seems to be gone now."

"Completely gone? There's nothing left?"

He continued to gaze upward as if he could find answers there. "I can almost see their faces. A man— tanned, brown hair, blue eyes, a darker blue than my own. And a teenage girl. Red hair. Big, bright eyes. A smile that lights up a room."

"They sound nice."

"I think they are—if they even exist," he added in a growl, rolling to sit on the side of the bed.

"Of course they exist. They're obviously memories—friends or relatives. People who mean something to you."

"Maybe. I've got to get ready for work."

"You're going to work *now?* Sam, you could be on the verge of a breakthrough."

"And I could be on the verge of a killer headache," he replied. "That's what usually results from trying to push too hard to remember."

"Did you tell Dr. Frank about those headaches?" she asked, laying a hand on his shoulder.

"I told him. He put it in my chart for the neurologist to study."

"So you're just going to work."

"Right. Maybe more memories will return, maybe they won't, but Bill Pollard's going to want his ham and eggs and coffee."

Serena sighed and pushed a hand through her tousled hair. There were times when she just didn't understand this man at all.

Sam went through the motions of his job with almost mechanical efficiency that day. Business was brisk, and the atmosphere in the diner was pleasant and friendly. Though he doubted that waiting tables was his usual job, he actually enjoyed his stint here. He'd made friends and had felt useful and productive. He would miss being here when he was lying on a couch in some shrink's office or sitting in a padded cell or wherever they stashed patients with Swiss-cheese minds.

The people he'd recalled that morning—Shane and Molly, whoever they were—seemed to indicate that his memories weren't lost, only suppressed. And that they were beginning to surface. At least, that was the way Serena seemed to interpret it.

Maybe she was right. By this time next week he could be back in his old life, working in whatever job he usually held, interacting with people who were only fuzzy images to him now, answering to a different name. Maybe he had loved that life. Maybe he would again. But he suspected he would always miss this place.

"Are you doing okay, Sam?" Marjorie asked at one point during the lunch rush.

"I'm fine," he assured her, wryly amused by her

dramatic stage whisper. They had agreed not to tell anyone else about his amnesia—at least, not yet.

"You let me know if you need anything," she said, patting his arm on her way to her post at the cash register. Both the gesture and her tone were quite maternal.

Thinking of his suspicions that he'd had a less than ideal childhood, he wondered what his own mother had been like. Marjorie Schaffer was exactly what he would have wanted in a mother, had he been given a choice.

As the time drew nearer to closing, Sam glanced at the glass front of the diner to see if any stragglers were on their way in. He froze for a moment when he spotted a man standing on the sidewalk outside. Tall, straight, rather stiff—buttoned down, he thought. What were the odds that Sam had seen him before, at the Independence Day celebration?

On an impulse, he started to move toward the door. Maybe this guy could answer a few questions…

"Hey, Sam. Can I get some coffee here?" someone called.

Hesitating for only a moment, Sam turned toward the kitchen. He was still on duty—and he didn't know what he'd have said to the guy, anyway.

By the time the front door was locked and the Open sign flipped around to the Closed side, whoever Sam had spotted outside appeared to be long gone. He hadn't come inside; he seemed to have been looking the place over.

Watching *him?* Sam couldn't help wondering.

It was his turn to haul the garbage bags out to the Dumpster in the alley behind the diner. Swapping jokes with his co-workers, he gathered the bags in both arms and stepped out the back door. The door closed behind him.

It must have been instinct that made the hairs on the back of his neck suddenly stand on end. There hadn't been a sound. His reflexive flinch made the blow that was intended for his head fall across his shoulders, instead.

He hit the ground, then rolled, ignoring the pain, gathering his strength. He wasn't sure whether he'd had a chance to fight back last time he was attacked, but he wouldn't go down easily this time.

The man he'd spotted on the Fourth of July stood over him, holding a steel bar. He swung it again at almost the same moment Sam recognized him, the vicious blow aimed for Sam's face.

Sam rolled again, feeling the whoosh of air as the bar missed him by less than an inch. He bumped into one of the plastic garbage bags he'd dropped, halting his momentum, trapping him while his attacker lifted the bar again.

With a grunt of effort, Sam kicked out, his foot landing solidly on the guy's knee. Though his sneaker wasn't as effective as a heavy boot would have been, the kick was effective, making the other guy stumble backward long enough to give Sam a chance to shove himself to his feet.

He remembered how to fight, he discovered in the next few tense moments, but fists were little defense against a thick steel bar wielded by someone who obviously knew what to do with it. The bar landed solidly against his upper left arm, making him numb to his fingertips, and then across his ribs, which hadn't fully healed from the last beating. The pain took his breath away. It was mostly desperation and blind luck that allowed him to get in a teeth-rattling blow of his own, right against the other guy's jaw.

Snarling in rage, the guy lifted the bar again, muscles bulging in his arms with the force of his movement. Sam braced himself.

A furious, almost animalistic growl signaled the arrival of help. In a blur of movement, a man plowed into Sam's attacker, knocking the guy flat on his face on the pavement. The bar clattered as it fell from his hand. Sam kicked it out of the way, then dove into the struggle to subdue the guy, who was fighting wildly to escape the new arrival.

The back door opened. "Sam?" It was Marjorie's voice. "Are you ready to—"

"Call the police!" Sam shouted, wanting her inside and out of any possibility of danger.

A moment later, he was sitting on the attacker's legs while his rescuer restrained the guy's arms. Sam looked at the new arrival and recognized the face as one out of his dreams. "Shane?" he asked tentatively.

"No, it's Santa Claus," Shane drawled sarcastically. "What the hell have you gotten yourself into this time, Cam?"

Cam. The name sounded familiar, though it didn't bring a blinding flash of revelation with it.

Dan arrived very quickly, accompanied by the two uniformed officers Sam had met before. After a few minutes of pandemonium, during which the attacker refused to utter a word, the cops left with their prisoner, and the diner employees rather reluctantly cleared out, leaving Marjorie, Sam and Shane in the place. Until that point, adrenaline had kept Sam on his feet, hardly aware of the pain of his latest injuries. Now he felt every one, particularly in his ribs and across his back where the first strike had landed, the one intended to knock him unconscious and render him helpless to follow-up blows.

He felt himself swaying on his feet and reached out to grab the back of a chair to steady himself.

"You okay, buddy?" Looking every inch the lanky cowboy, Shane placed his hands on his lean, denim-covered hips and studied him closely.

Sam drew a deep breath. "I, uh, I'm afraid I don't remember you, exactly," he admitted. "But thanks for the help out there."

Shane's dark blue eyes narrowed in confusion. "You don't remember me? But you called me by name."

Sam shrugged. The automatic movement sent cascades of pain from his shoulders to the pit of his stomach. He felt the room starting to sway around him. "Damn," he muttered. "Looks like I'm going to be visiting Dr. Frank again."

He heard Marjorie cry out and Shane exclaim something before he hit the floor. After that, he heard nothing.

Chapter Fifteen

Serena hurried down the hospital hallway with a disturbing sense of déjà vu. Without remembering to knock, she pushed open the door she'd been directed to and rushed into the room. Sam sat on the side of the bed, and there was another man in a chair close by. Judging from their expressions, they'd obviously been engaged in a serious conversation.

"Are you all right?" she asked when Sam turned to look at her.

"I'm okay. Just a few new bruises to add to that patchwork quilt," he quipped, holding out a hand to her.

She placed her hand in his and was somewhat reassured by the strength of his grip. There were no fresh bruises on his face, as far as she could tell, but he held himself rather stiffly, turning his head with caution.

"You really have to stop doing things like this," she chided him gruffly. "You can't take too much more."

"It isn't as if I've tried to get run down and beaten up," he retorted. "I just seem to be good at being in the wrong place at the wrong time."

Serena looked at the other man, who'd been watching them with obvious interest. Sam made the introductions. "Serena Schaffer, this is Shane Walker."

"Shane," she repeated, feeling her eyes go wide. "You're Shane?"

"Nice to meet you, ma'am," he said in an unmistakable Texas drawl. "Cam's been telling me about how kind you and your mother have been to him."

"Cam?" she parroted, not quite sure she'd heard correctly.

The man she had known as Sam Wallace nodded, his expression devoid of emotion. "Apparently, my name is Cameron North and I'm a reporter with a Dallas newspaper."

Her knees weakened. She sank to the bed beside Sam—Cameron, she corrected herself—before she embarrassed herself by folding to the floor. "Cameron North," she repeated, testing the sound of it.

"We've been concerned about Cam since he disappeared three weeks ago," Shane explained, looking from his friend to Serena. "I knew he was pursuing a story that had some danger involved and I was afraid that something had happened to him. I've got a couple of uncles who are private investigators, and they've been looking for him. When Chief Meadows sent out a report about a John Doe matching Cam's description showing up here in Edstown, I had to come check it out. A few questions led me to the diner, where I found Cameron involved in a brawl out back."

Serena looked at Cameron. "Do you remember anything?"

He shrugged. "Some of what Shane's been telling me sounds familiar. A few memories have surfaced, but they're still pretty patchy."

"I've promised we'll get him the best medical help," Shane said. "I've got another couple of uncles who are doctors in Dallas."

"An uncle for every occasion," Cameron murmured, and the dry remark sounded so much like Sam that Serena's throat tightened. Maybe he had a different name now, but he was still the man she'd tumbled so recklessly in love with during the past three weeks.

"Shane thinks it will be good for me to go back to Dallas, check out my usual haunts there. He thinks the memories will come back faster in my natural element."

"He's probably right," Serena agreed reluctantly. "You'd probably recover faster at home."

"Home." Sam—or rather Cameron, she corrected herself again—said the word as if he'd never heard it before. "Funny. When I think of home, it isn't Dallas. It's the guest house."

A pang went through her heart. She looked at their joined hands, wondering if she would ever be able to step into the guest house again or if her memories would be too overwhelming. Something told her she would welcome a bit of amnesia after he was gone—but she knew she would remember every minute she'd spent with him.

"Your family must be frantic about you," she murmured. *And please don't let that family include a wife or kids,* she added silently.

Shane cleared his throat. "Actually, Cam's not really close to his parents. I doubt they know he's been gone. He's always said that he's closer to my family than his own."

"That must be why he couldn't tell whether you were a friend or a brother when he remembered you."

Shane gave his friend a faint smile. "Yeah. Must be."

She noticed that Shane wore a wedding ring. "I see you're married. Is your wife's name Molly?"

"No, Molly's my sister," Shane replied, confirming Cameron's guess from that morning. "My wife's name is Kelly."

"I'm not married," Cameron told her, as if he guessed her biggest fear. "Never have been, according to Shane."

Shane chuckled. "You've never even come close," he said. "Not that there haven't been quite a few who tried to change your mind."

Serena didn't smile. She noticed that Cameron didn't, either. "When are you leaving?"

His eyes were somber when he answered. "Shane has a plane waiting at the airport in Little Rock. We can leave immediately."

"One of my cousins is a pilot," Shane murmured.

"Of course," she replied. "You, uh, have a large family, I take it?"

"Larger than you can probably imagine." He stood. "I'll go call my cousin and make the arrangements for our trip home. I'm sure you two have a few things to say to each other. And, uh, Cam—" He paused in the doorway.

"Yes?"

"Don't be an idiot."

"What did he mean by that?" Serena asked when the other man had disappeared into the hallway.

"Apparently he has a rather warped sense of humor. I haven't caught up with it yet."

"Mother told me what happened. Have you found out who it was that attacked you?"

"Shane's pretty sure he's someone who works for the guy I was investigating for an exposé—a public official I suspected of using embezzled tax money to provide a lavish lifestyle for his wife and kids in Dallas and an equally extravagant existence for a mistress in Little Rock. Before I left Texas, I told Shane I would be in Little Rock, pursuing my hunches. Apparently, I was caught snooping."

"You think whoever beat you up thought you were dead when they dumped you here in Edstown?"

He shrugged. "That's a reasonable guess. If you hadn't found me, I would have been dead by morning."

She swallowed. "And does Shane think you're still in danger?"

"No. Shane had his P.I. uncles follow up on my leads. They've found evidence that I was right all along. Once the story breaks, there will be no further incentive to try to get rid of me. And Dan will probably get a confession out of the guy who jumped me this afternoon, some sort of deal that implicates his employer and lessens his own punishment."

"So you're going back to Dallas now to solve a new mystery," she said. "Your own, this time."

He lifted a shoulder. "I guess that sums it up. How would you like to go along? You could be Dr. Watson to my Holmes."

He made it sound like a joke, but something told

her he was partially serious. Though she was flattered to think he wanted to take her with him, she couldn't help wondering if he was merely clinging to a familiar lifeline in an understandably overwhelming situation.

Besides, she thought sadly, she wasn't Kara. Serena couldn't just drop everything and run off with a gorgeous male on a quest of his own. "I'm afraid that won't be possible," she said, trying to speak lightly. "I have a few responsibilities here—a law practice, a newspaper, a mother, a dog. Unless you want to take the dog with you?" she offered with a valiant attempt at humor.

"I don't think Walter would care for Dallas. He's a small-town dog."

"You're probably right." And she was a small-town girl. Some facts just had to be faced, no matter how difficult.

There was a heavy moment of silence and then Cameron spoke again. "Shane said money isn't really a problem for me, so I won't have any trouble paying my medical bills or the money I owe you and your mother. Apparently, I come from a distinguished line of attorneys, and I've been fondly remembered by my late grandparents."

"Attorneys?" She remembered his distinctly negative reaction to the profession.

"Yeah. I guess even rich lawyers have been known to slap their kids around."

"You still don't remember your parents?"

"No. But Shane promised to give me all the unhappy details during the flight to Dallas."

"Shane will probably be back in a minute."

He looked toward the door. "Very likely."

She stood and turned to face him, cupping his face

between her hands. "Before he gets back—" Leaning closer, she spoke with her lips just brushing his. "I'll miss you, Sam Wallace."

"I'll miss *being* Sam Wallace," he confessed. "He's a pretty happy guy. I'm not so sure about Cameron North."

Because she didn't know how to respond to that, she covered his lips with hers. She didn't know about Cameron North, either, but she suspected she could love him just as easily as she had fallen for Sam Wallace—had things been different for them, of course.

It was hot. Arkansas in August hot. And Serena was miserable. But then, she'd been in that condition for more than a month, and her mood had little to do with the weather. She'd been depressed since Sam—*Cameron,* she corrected herself irritably—had gone to Dallas with his friend Shane.

He'd called a few times during the first couple of weeks after he left, keeping her updated about his progress in regaining his memory. Time and therapy had been productive; he'd recovered a great deal, though there were still gaps that the doctors said might never be completely filled. Cameron hadn't seemed as concerned about that as Serena might have expected him to be. As a matter of fact, he hadn't seemed particularly emotional about anything—being home, being reunited with his friends, receiving praise for his part in uncovering a political scandal.

She'd been disturbed by the detached, impassive tone he'd used over the telephone. Maybe that was the way Cameron North always spoke. It wasn't the way she remembered Sam Wallace.

It had been almost three weeks since he'd last

called. She assumed he'd been too busy reclaiming his life. He didn't owe her any more calls, of course. They'd made no promises, no plans for the future. What they'd shared had been very special, but they'd known all along it was temporary. She'd been a port in the storm for him, and he'd given her a chance to be reckless and irresponsible for once in her neatly programmed life. Each of them had performed their role well; she couldn't say now that she'd ever expected more.

But, damn, she missed him.

She pushed her limp hair off her face, scowling as she thought again about how hot it was. She sat in the editor's office of the *Evening Star,* a daunting pile of paperwork in front of her. The central air-conditioning unit was old and unreliable. It needed to be replaced, but she wasn't sure the dwindling budget could justify that this year. And she couldn't guarantee that the paper would still be in operation next summer—not unless she found someone who could rectify the poor business decisions Marvin had made during the past couple of years. Someone who knew the publishing business, understood small-town politics and was willing to work long hours for a rather meager salary.

She'd been searching in vain for a managing editor since she'd finally given in to the inevitable and fired Marvin two weeks earlier. He'd gone more easily than she'd expected, having already realized that he could no longer perform his job. To everyone's relief, he'd decided to get some help with his drinking and then move to Florida to live closer to his only brother. Until a replacement could be found, Riley and Lindsey were trying to help Serena keep things afloat, but there were times when it felt as if they were fighting a losing battle.

Rubbing her temples, she glanced at that day's edition, which was spread on one corner of the desk. The lead story had to do with a breakthrough in the recent rash of break-ins, such as the ones in which Cameron had been implicated. Dan had finally found evidence that Delbert Farley was, indeed, involved in the crimes, along with an accomplice from a neighboring town. Delbert's girlfriend, Rita Hinson, was being charged as an accessory to the burglaries. Young Zach was in the custody of child welfare services. Serena hoped the boy would end up in a better environment than he'd endured thus far in his short life.

The image of an unhappy boy brought her thoughts back to Cameron. *Everything* seemed to bring him to her mind. She closed her eyes and rested her elbows on the desk, wondering if she would ever stop thinking about him.

Was this why Kara had been willing to leave her whole life behind to follow Pierce to Nashville? Because she would rather risk heartbreak with him than to live with the emptiness without him?

For the first time, Serena was beginning to understand her sister's actions. She still couldn't see herself walking away from all the responsibilities she'd taken on—well, most of the time, anyway—but she no longer criticized Kara for following her heart. Serena wanted her sister to be happy. And there were times—mostly in the middle of sleepless nights—when she wondered what it would be like to follow her sister's example.

''I understand you're looking for a managing editor.''

The familiar male voice brought Serena's head up with such a jerk that she nearly fell out of her chair. Her eyes wide, she stared at the doorway. "Sam?"

His golden hair trimmed and brushed, his face free of bruises, his elegantly slender body clad in an expensive-looking gray suit, he leaned against the door-jamb wearing an enigmatic smile that didn't quite reach his piercing blue eyes. "You can call me that if you like. I also answer to Cam or Cameron."

She couldn't quite seem to find the strength to stand up. "What are you doing here?"

"May I come in?"

"Of course. What are you *doing* here?"

He closed the office door behind him. "You know, if I'd ever visited you at this office while I was in town, I might have recovered a few memories more quickly. There's just something about a newspaper office, no matter what the size of the operation—"

"S— Cam, you're driving me crazy. Are you going to tell me why you're here?"

"I'm here to apply for the managing editor position." He tossed something on the desk in front of her. "That's my résumé. I think you'll find that I'm qualified."

He was joking—he had to be. She refused to allow herself to believe he was serious. "If you're here to pay whatever debt you think you owe me or my mother, forget it. We both told you that you don't owe us anything."

"That's not exactly true, but it's not why I'm here. I'm completely serious, Serena. I want the job."

"But—"

He took the seat across the desk from her, sitting straight and still, looking uncharacteristically formal.

"I realize that you don't really know Cameron North, so I understand if you want to conduct an interview before you make your decision. Ask me anything you like. Or would you rather I just start talking?"

Her brain seemed to have temporarily forgotten how to function. "I don't—"

"Okay, I'll do the talking." He drew a deep breath. "I'm thirty-five, single and currently unemployed, since I quit my job with the newspaper in Dallas. I'm in generally good health, though I've got some large, fuzzy gaps in my memories that may or may not clear up with passing time. I've spent the past few years working too hard, drinking too much and sulking about my dysfunctional family. I've let my bitterness hurt people—nice women who wanted more from me than I was willing or able to give them, good friends who have worried about my self-destructive habits."

"You, uh, might want to work on your interview skills," Serena advised shakily. "You're supposed to be convincing me to hire you, not discouraging me from doing so."

"I thought I should give you the negatives first, just so there'd be no worry that I tried to deceive you."

She cleared her throat, feeling strength flood her limbs again, along with a surge of exhilaration. "And the positives?"

"I'm a hard worker. I know the newspaper business. I'm ready for new challenges. You won't have to worry about me leaving for greener pastures. I've been around enough to know there aren't any."

"I find it rather hard to believe you've always dreamed of running a small-town newspaper," she whispered, her eyes locked on his face.

"No. I always dreamed of finding a place to call

home," he answered quietly. "I just didn't know where to look before."

"There's not a lot to do around here. How do I know you won't get bored?"

The faintest smile quirked the corner of his mouth. "I wouldn't say it gets boring around here. There's dancing at Gaylord's. Wrestling on big-screen TV at the pizza parlor. Thirty-six flavors of snow cones. And I never got a chance to go parking down by the lake on a Saturday night."

"Those things are enough to keep you here permanently?"

"No." He stood and walked slowly around the corner of the desk. Leaning over her chair, he tipped her chin back and lowered his mouth to within an inch of hers. "But you are."

She lifted to meet him, trying to express in her kiss exactly how much she had missed him while he'd been gone. Judging from the enthusiastic way he gathered her into his arms, pulling her out of her chair and onto her tiptoes, he had missed her, too.

Locking her arms around his neck, she pressed herself so tightly against him that there was no separation left between them. Exactly the way she wanted it.

He released her mouth to give them both a chance to breathe, resting his forehead against hers. "I've missed you. So much I ached with it—worse than I ever ached from any physical injuries."

"I missed you, too," she whispered. "Every time I looked at the guest house, every time I sat in the rose garden, every time I ate in the diner, all I could think about was how empty it seemed without you there. It seemed hard to believe you'd only been here three weeks. Everywhere I looked, you were there."

"With every memory I recovered in Dallas, I was only more convinced that I'd never been happier than I was during those three weeks here," he answered unsteadily. "I kept telling myself you didn't really know me, that you couldn't possibly feel the way about me that I did about you, that you deserved someone better—but I couldn't stay away."

"You don't know how many times I thought about coming to Dallas to find you. Maybe to drag you back here—or maybe I would have stayed with you. I don't know. I guess I'm more like my sister than I've wanted to admit."

"I want to meet your sister—and her singing beau."

"I want you to meet them. And I want to meet anyone who's important to you."

"We'll invite them all to the wedding. Hell, we'll even invite my parents, if they aren't too busy with their own pursuits to spare the time. I want you to know everything about me—good and bad. I want you to know me the way no one else ever has—not even Shane, who's been my best friend since we were teenagers."

She traced a finger along his jaw. His face was so dearly familiar to her, whatever name he used. "We've known each other such a short time, and already you're talking about a wedding. There are people who will say we're crazy."

He laughed. "They won't be calling me anything I haven't called myself this summer. But take if from someone who knows—crazy isn't as bad as it sounds."

Her smile felt big enough to split her face. "Let's be crazy together, Cameron North."

He kissed her lingeringly, then lifted his head with a grin. "Does this mean I got the job?"

"You're hired. Now can we get out of here?"

He wrapped an arm around her shoulders. "We could always go park by the lake," he suggested as they moved together toward the door.

"I have a better idea," she said, taking his hand. "Let's go find a bed."

"You're right. That *is* a better idea." He reached eagerly for the doorknob.

Epilogue

"I never thought I would live to see this day," Shane commented, amusement and approval evident in his deep voice.

"Hey, you're the one who's been nagging me for years to settle down and get married," Cameron reminded him.

"Yeah. But since when did you ever take my advice?"

Cameron chuckled and glanced across the room where his new bride accepted hugs and kisses from a seemingly endless stream of local well-wishers. With all her friends in Edstown and his from Dallas, there had been quite a large audience to witness the exchange of vows. The reception hall was crowded, just as tiny Edstown Baptist Church had been filled almost to the rafters for the ceremony. Shane said that was a good sign—lots of witnesses to make sure Cameron kept his word.

Cameron knew he wouldn't have changed his mind had no one showed up but him and Serena and the preacher.

"Kelly approves of your choice, by the way," Shane remarked. "She's already quite fond of Serena. As much as I regret having you move so far away from Dallas, I have a feeling we'll be getting together often."

"Every chance we get," Cameron promised.

He was glad that Shane's wife and their other friends liked Serena. It touched him that they'd all made an effort to be with him today—Scott and Lydia Pearson coming all the way from Florida and more than a dozen others from the Dallas area. His friends had stood up with him—Shane the best man, of course, Scott Pearson and Michael Chang his groomsmen. Shane's father, Jared, had come, along with his wife, Cassie, and young Molly. Shane's cousin Brynn and her husband, Dr. Joe D'Alessandro, were there, as well, along with a few of Shane's other numerous relatives. They'd all been so much a part of his past; he was glad they were there to watch him take a giant step toward an even better future.

Cameron's parents had attended the ceremony, looking more like strangers who just happened to be seated beside each other than proud and happy parents, but they hadn't stayed for the reception. They'd claimed other obligations. Cameron knew they had no interest in attending this gathering of people they considered their social inferiors. Their attitude no longer had the power to hurt him. He had Serena by his side now—and they had agreed that their own children, if any, would never have any reason to doubt that their parents loved them—and each other.

"I can see why you like it here," Shane said, looking around the room at the chattering cluster of wedding guests. "It seems like a nice, friendly place."

Cameron nodded, his gaze on his radiant-looking bride. The residents of Edstown were quite nice, but it was Serena who made him want to stay here. He had a feeling he'd like any place she called home.

It turned out he was the one who had something in common with her sister, Kara, who had served as Serena's maid of honor. Both Cameron and Kara had been willing to walk away from the lives they'd known to be with the ones they loved. In a private conversation a couple of hours before the wedding ceremony, they'd agreed that neither of them had any regrets.

"Congratulations, Sam—I mean, Cam. You got yourself a fine woman there." Bill Pollard thumped Cameron heartily on the shoulder as he spoke. The locals had accepted his amnesia more readily than he could have expected, but they were still having a little trouble getting used to his new name.

Maybe Cameron was developing a callus or something on that shoulder. He no longer flinched when Bill exchanged his usual hearty greeting. "Thanks, Bill."

"And the paper's looking real good since you took over," the older man added. "'Course, I do miss you over at the diner. Your coffee was even better than Justine's."

"Don't let her hear you say that. She'll snatch you bald-headed."

Chuckling, Bill thumped him again, then headed

off, saying over his shoulder, "You got that right. See you around, S— Cam."

Shane laughed. "Yeah. I can tell you're going to fit in around here just fine."

Cameron's attention had already strayed. Serena was making her way across the room to him, extending her hand when she reached him. He took it tightly in his own.

"It's a lovely reception, isn't it?" she asked as Shane moved discreetly away.

"Lovely. Can we leave now? I want to make love to my wife," Cameron informed her, lifting her hand to his lips.

"You'll have to be patient a little while longer. Mother's going to insist that I throw the bouquet. Molly wants to catch it, but Shane's vowed to body check her if he has to. He doesn't want to even think about her getting married for another ten years or so."

Cameron sighed. "I'll give you another half hour. Then we're out of here."

She smiled brightly at him. "Sounds good to me."

"I love you, Serena."

"I love you, too." She leaned her head against his shoulder. "How did we ever get along without each other?"

He grinned. "I couldn't say. I seem to have forgotten everything that happened to me before I met you."

She sighed in response to the bad joke, then lifted her face for his kiss.

Cameron could have told her that he hadn't been entirely joking. As far as he was concerned, the most important part of his life had begun the day he'd opened his eyes and had first seen Serena's face.

It wasn't Edstown that was his Brigadoon, he realized. It was Serena, herself. Her love had entrapped him—and he never wanted to leave.

* * * * *

SILHOUETTE®
MAKES YOU
A STAR!

Feel like a star with Silhouette.

We will fly you and a guest to New York City for an exciting weekend stay at a glamorous 5-star hotel. Experience a refreshing day at one of New York's trendiest spas and have your photo taken by a professional. Plus, receive $1,000 U.S. spending money!

Flowers...long walks...dinner for two... how does Silhouette Books make romance come alive for you?

Send us a script, with 500 words or less, along with visuals (only drawings, magazine cutouts or photographs or combination thereof). Show us how Silhouette Makes Your Love Come Alive. Be creative and have fun. No purchase necessary. All entries must be clearly marked with your name, address and telephone number. All entries will become property of Silhouette and are not returnable. **Contest closes September 28, 2001.**

Please send your entry to: **Silhouette Makes You a Star!**

In U.S.A.	In Canada
P.O. Box 9069	P.O. Box 637
Buffalo, NY, 14269-9069	Fort Erie, ON, L2A 5X3

Look for contest details on the next page, by visiting www.eHarlequin.com or request a copy by sending a self-addressed envelope to the applicable address above. Contest open to Canadian and U.S. residents who are 18 or over. Void where prohibited.

Silhouette®
Where love comes alive™

Our lucky winner's photo will appear in a Silhouette ad. Join the fun!

SRMYAS1

HARLEQUIN "SILHOUETTE MAKES YOU A STAR!" CONTEST 1308
OFFICIAL RULES
NO PURCHASE NECESSARY TO ENTER

1. To enter, follow directions published in the offer to which you are responding. Contest begins June 1, 2001, and ends on September 28, 2001. Entries must be postmarked by September 28, 2001, and received by October 5, 2001. Enter by hand-printing (or typing) on an 8 ½" x 11" piece of paper your name, address (including zip code), contest number/name and attaching a script containing <u>500 words or less, along with drawings, photographs or magazine cutouts, or combinations thereof</u> (i.e., collage) <u>on no larger than 9" x 12"</u> piece of paper, describing how the Silhouette books make romance come alive for you. Mail via first-class mail to: Harlequin "Silhouette Makes You a Star!" Contest 1308, (in the U.S.) P.O. Box 9069, Buffalo, NY 14269-9069, (in Canada) P.O. Box 637, Fort Erie, Ontario, Canada L2A 5X3. Limit one entry per person, household or organization.

2. Contests will be judged by a panel of members of the Harlequin editorial, marketing and public relations staff. Fifty percent of criteria will be judged against script and fifty percent will be judged against drawing, photographs and/or magazine cutouts. Judging criteria will be based on the following.

   - Sincerity—25%
   - Originality and Creativity—50%
   - Emotionally Compelling—25%

   In the event of a tie, duplicate prizes will be awarded. Decisions of the judges are final.

3. All entries become the property of Torstar Corp. and may be used for future promotional purposes. Entries will not be returned. No responsibility is assumed for lost, late, illegible, incomplete, inaccurate, nondelivered or misdirected mail.

4. Contest open only to residents of the U.S. <u>(except Puerto Rico)</u> and Canada who are 18 years of age or older, and is void wherever prohibited by law; all applicable laws and regulations apply. Any litigation within the Province of Quebec respecting the conduct or organization of a publicity contest may be submitted to the Régie des alcools, des courses et des jeux for a ruling. Any litigation respecting the awarding of a prize may be submitted to the Régie des alcools, des courses et des jeux only for the purpose of helping the parties reach a settlement. Employees and immediate family members of Torstar Corp. and D. L. Blair, Inc., their affiliates, subsidiaries and all other agencies, entities and persons connected with the use, marketing or conduct of this contest are not eligible to enter. Taxes on prizes are the sole responsibility of the winner. Acceptance of any prize offered constitutes permission to use winner's name, photograph or other likeness for the purposes of advertising, trade and promotion on behalf of Torstar Corp., its affiliates and subsidiaries without further compensation to the winner, unless prohibited by law.

5. Winner will be determined no later than November 30, 2001, and will be notified by mail. Winner will be required to sign and return an Affidavit of Eligibility/Release of Liability/Publicity Release form within 15 days after winner notification. Noncompliance within that time period may result in disqualification and an alternative winner may be selected. All travelers must execute a Release of Liability prior to ticketing and must possess required travel documents (e.g., passport, photo ID) where applicable. Trip must be booked by December 31, 2001, and completed within one year of notification. No substitution of prize permitted by winner. Torstar Corp. and D. L. Blair, Inc., their parents, affiliates and subsidiaries are not responsible for errors in printing of contest, entries and/or game pieces. In the event of printing or other errors that may result in unintended prize values or duplication of prizes, all affected game pieces or entries shall be null and void. **Purchase or acceptance of a product offer does not improve your chances of winning.**

6. Prizes: (1) Grand Prize—A 2-night/3-day trip for two (2) to New York City, including round-trip coach air transportation nearest winner's home and hotel accommodations (double occupancy) at The Plaza Hotel, a glamorous afternoon makeover at <u>a trendy New York spa</u>, $1,000 in U.S. spending money and an opportunity to <u>have a professional photo taken and appear in a Silhouette advertisement</u> (approximate retail value: $7,000). (10) Ten Runner-Up Prizes of gift packages (retail value $50 ea.). Prizes consist of only those items listed as part of the prize. Limit one prize per person. Prize is valued in U.S. currency.

7. For the name of the winner (available after December 31, 2001) send a self-addressed, stamped envelope to: Harlequin "Silhouette Makes You a Star!" Contest 1197 Winners, P.O. Box 4200 Blair, NE 68009-4200 or you may access the www.eHarlequin.com Web site through February 28, 2002.

Contest sponsored by Torstar Corp., P.O Box 9042, Buffalo, NY 14269-9042.

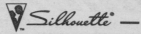

**Don't miss this exciting new
Silhouette Special Edition
series from Laurie Paige!**

Twenty years ago, tragedy
struck the Windoms. Now the
truth will be revealed with the
power—and passion—of true
love! Meet Kate, Shannon
and Megan, three cousins who
vow to restore the family name.

THE
**WINDRAVEN
LEGACY**

On sale May 2001
A stranger came, looking for a place to stay—
but what was he really looking for…? Find out why
Kate has **SOMETHING TO TALK ABOUT.**

On sale July 2001
An accident robbed Shannon of her sight, but a
neighbor refused to let her stay blind about her
feelings…in **WHEN I SEE YOUR FACE.**

On sale September 2001
Megan's memories of childhood had been lost.
Now she has a chance to discover the truth about
love…**WHEN I DREAM OF YOU.**

Available at your favorite retail outlet.

Silhouette®
Where love comes alive™